PRETTY GURLS LOVE HUSTLAS

NIDDA

TEXT UCP TO 22828 TO SUBSCRIBE TO OUR
MAILING LIST
If you would like to join our team, submit the first 3-4
chapters of your completed manuscript to
Submissions@UrbanChapterspublications.com

ACKNOWLEDGMENTS

First, I would like to thank God. This writing journey has not been easy, but every time that I think about giving up it's you that gives me the strength to keep going. Now, I'm here at book 10 and I didn't think I could do it but I got it done! Next my family for being supportive and always rooting for me even when I'm not doing it for myself! I truly appreciate the ones that have rocked with me from day one Keyah and Rani! Y'all words they might have seemed little to y'all, but I have to say that y'all have motivated me so many times to keep going! I would like to also give a big shout out to Trenae'. Check out her books if you haven't. From day one she was always willing to help me. Coming into this game I didn't know much, and she genuinely was willing to answer any questions, offer advice, listen to story lines and help any way that she can. Me being me, I'm really picky about those that I even talk to in this industry and out, but I truly appreciate your help!

KEEP UP WITH ME

Facebook: Nidda Bidda
Instagram: Authornidda
Twitter: _Nidda__

1

RICARDO MATTHEWS

R'Shad can sleep through anything. I can't believe he still sleeping the way that momma is screaming. It's almost time for us to get up for school, but I couldn't sleep until the alarm went off. Every morning when my dad, Reggie, gets off work, it's the same shit. They be on this shit every morning, and I'm sick of it. I can't wait to get the fuck out of this house.

"You shut the fuck up. I'm grown. Yo' kids is down the hall. If you want to tell somebody what the fuck they can and can't do, I suggest you tell them!" My momma, Carmen, screamed.

"You a disrespectful ass bitch! After all the shit that I've done for you!" Reggie screamed back louder than my momma.

"Done, for me? As in the past tense, muthafucka. What have you done for me lately?" My momma screamed.

Laying in my bed, I couldn't help but think back to

the times when shit wasn't all fucked up in our house. A few minutes passed and shit got quiet throughout the house. They weren't arguing no more, but before I knew it, a bunch of shit started hitting the floor. I already knew what the fuck was going on, even with me not being in the room with them.

This shit has made me hate him. I can't believe when I was younger I wanted to be just like that nigga. This is something that has been going on for a few months too damn long. Every time he leaves, I just wish his ass would never come back. Then every morning, his drunk ass shows up back here.

I couldn't hear momma screaming or my dad yelling anymore, so they must be done for this morning. I made my way to the bathroom to get in the shower, so we can get to the bus stop on time today. I jumped in the shower and I could hear my mom screaming for R'Shad to get up. Most people my age, hate going to school but to be able to get out this house shit I can't wait to get to school. After about thirty minutes and R'Shad banging on the bathroom door, I got out the shower and made my way into our room. My mom had Foot Locker bags on the floor at the foot of both of our beds.

"Good morning, baby," my mom said as she hugged me tight.

My mother is so beautiful. She has dark skin, light brown eyes and long, silky black hair. Even with the busted lip that Reggie must have given her earlier, she still keeps it pushing and makes sure that my brother and I are always good. My momma is my heart, and I don't know what I would do without her. Reggie used to pay the bills and make sure we are good, but lately his punk ass ain't been doing nothing for us. He goes to work, drinks, and it's no secret that he be out here tricking with bitches.

"R'Shad, get the fuck up and get ready for school. You don't know what the fuck I went through to get the money to buy these shoes and shit for y'all!" Momma screamed.

"Momma, I'm up. I'm up," R'Shad said, pulling the covers from over his head.

"Nigga, it took you long enough. I know yo light skin ass heard me knocking on the fucking door!" R'Shad spat as he made his way to the bathroom.

We both know what momma did to get the money. It's not a secret what my momma be doing when Reggie leave to go to work. We don't talk about it and act like the shit ain't happening, just like we don't talk about the fact that Reggie come in here and beat her ass every day.

"Today better be a good fucking day. I don't want no bullshit today. Y'all all the fuck y'all got. Never let nothing or nobody ever come in between y'all. Not even that lil bitch, Felica, R'Shad!" Momma yelled.

The respect that I once had for Reggie went away after I seen him put his hands on my momma. I'll be lying if I said dealing with this shit is easy, but I just do what the fuck I got to do. Dealing with the bullshit in this house ain't easy for me, but it's even harder for R'Shad. R'Shad got up and made his way out the room. Momma flopped down on R'Shad's bed as I brushed my hair.

"I'm good, don't worry about me. I got us, and I'm going to make sure we are good," Momma said.

I didn't respond. I just nodded my head. My momma is the strongest woman that I know and no matter what, nothing will ever change that. Having to do everything on her own isn't easy, but R'Shad picks up where she lacks. Nobody outside this house will ever know what is going on and my momma makes sure of it. My momma won't even tell her sister or best friend and they know every damn thing else.

Being the youngest, me and my momma are close as fuck. To my momma, I will always be a baby even though I'm fourteen. She has to worry about R'Shad because he is always in some shit and stays getting kicked out of school. She knows she never has to worry about me when it comes to that shit. The only time I get in shit is when I'm with my brother because no matter what, I'll always have my brothers' back. My brother and momma are all I got, and nobody will ever come in between that.

Momma and I made our way downstairs while she told me the same shit she tells me every day. "Watch R'Shad because even though he's the oldest and is supposed to be watching you, he ain't got it all. That nigga kind of crazy," Momma said. That nigga stays on some bullshit and it's not a day that goes by that he isn't into it with some fucking body.

R'Shad finally made his way down the stairs so we could make it to the bus stop, running late like we do every morning. I jumped up off the couch so we could leave. Before we could get off the porch, momma was hollering.

"R' Shad, don't get yo' black ass kicked out of school today or I'm not coming to get ya ass!" My momma talks her shit, but whenever R'Shad does anything, she be right there to save his ass. Don't let nobody else try and say anything about R' Shad, her ass be ready to fight them.

"What's up, Scar?" Joey said as we walked up to the bus stop.

"Nigga, don't wassup up me. You already know what the fuck it is with me and you, bra," Scar spat. And by the look in his eyes, I knew he was ready for whatever.

I just hope that Joey chills and we don't have no shit this morning. Knowing my brother, it's going to be some shit sometime today. Just to be away from the house for a while, shit is good with me. I'll take R'Shad's shit over the shit with my momma and Reggie any day.

"Do Reggie work tonight?" Scar leaned over the seat to ask me.

"Shit, I hope so," I spat, sitting back and turning up Boosie in my headphones.

We pulled up to Felicia's bus stop and she got on the bus. You can't tell my brother shit about this bitch. She can't do no wrong in this nigga's eyes. My momma always says that it ain't gon' last long and he'll be on to the next bitch, but I don't think so. This nigga doesn't even talk about other bitches.

"Wassup, Ricardo?" Felicia said, and I didn't respond.

"Why don't yo' brother like me?" Felicia whined to Scar.

"He didn't hear you. He got his headphones in," Scar said, trying to make her feel better.

I don't like the bitch. She just a rat ass bitch that ain't gon' ever be shit but what she is now. My brother's mouth keeps him into shit, but this bitch makes it worse. Everyday this bitch got a problem. If a nigga looks at her too long, she coming to Scar about it. Him being the type of nigga he is, he not gon' let shit slide with anybody fuckin' with somebody he got love for. He got a scar on his face that proves how he's rocking for anybody that he down with.

R' SHAD "SCAR" MATTHEWS

As I threw the dice, before they hit the ground, I had my hand out to collect my money. The older niggas I was shooting with were mugging the fuck out us, but they handed over my muthafuckin' cash. I don't give a fuck how they feel, they gon' give me what's mine. To these niggas, this money don't mean shit, but this is how I made sure me and my little brother are always good. These same niggas every other day talk shit about me being young and how they gon' to take all my money. They ain't took shit that's mine but keep leaving short on they re-up money.

"Y'all better get in the house, it's dark out here." one of the niggas clowned.

"Nigga, I'll be back out here to take more of yo' shit nigga," I spat, opening up my juice and taking it to the head.

"Y'all niggas keep letting that lil nigga Scar take y'all fucking money," one of the niggas clowned.

I doubt these niggas even know my damn name. One

of the OG's started calling me Scar and that shit stuck; everybody calls me that now. Even though I'm sixteen, I've always hung with the older niggas.

We started on the walk around the corner to the house. I was already thinking about the J's I'm going to pick up in the morning. I'll be back in a few days to take some more of their fucking money.

"Momma ain't gon' never change," I spat, looking up across the street at our house.

There was a car in the driveway and that ain't our fucking car, Reggie still at work. I love my momma, but this shit is getting fucking old with these different niggas over here whenever Reggie ain't here. Between her, her damn company and Reggie's drunk ass, I can't wait to get me and Ricardo the fuck out this damn house.

"Sit right here while I go check this shit out," I said as Ricardo shook his head.

Leaving Ricardo on the porch, I made my way in the house to check shit out. The first thing I saw is my momma all in this nigga lap with her ass all out. This lil nigga that can't be much older than me, kissing and touching all over my fucking mom.

"For real, ma?"

My momma jumped up and straightened out her night gown. The nigga was looking at me crazy like I'm fucking up his nut.

"Where y'all been?" Momma asked as she walked up on me.

"You know that Reggie gon' come in here trippin'. Why you got this nigga in here?"

"I'm yo' momma. You not my daddy, R'Shad. My company is going to be gone before Reggie gets here,"

Momma said as she ran her hand across the scar on my face.

My momma always hollering to stay out her and Reggie shit, but I ain't trying to hear that. The scar on my face is from the first time I tried to stop Reggie from hitting my momma. He hit me so hard in my face, I was unconscious for hours. I don't give a fuck what nobody has to say, I'm not just gon' sit back while no mutha-fuckin' body putting his hands on my momma.

"Where is Ricardo at? I cooked. Go in there and eat, R'Shad. And stay out my damn business" Momma said as her and this young nigga made their way up the stairs.

I went to get Ricardo, and we made our way into the kitchen to eat. I ain't even surprised by that nigga being here; my momma stays on some bullshit. The bullshit that goes on in this house is why we stay away as much as we can. My momma always talking shit about us being in the streets, but don't nobody want to be here why some bitch ass nigga fucking my momma.

Making my plate, trying to get this bullshit off my mind, my stomach started growling. All this shit is happening because of Reggie's bitch ass. Ever since that nigga lost his job in construction, that nigga turned into a fucking drunk. It's his fucking fault for going to work drunk and being the reason other people got hurt. Instead of being a man and accepting what the fuck he did, he takes that shit out on my momma.

That nigga got another job, but the money he was seeing at first is long gone. That lil shit he's bringing in is barely keeping the lights on. Working with a temp service, some weeks he works all the damn time and others he doesn't. The project he'd been working on the past week is keeping him gone all the damn time, and that is when my momma gets on her bullshit. We finished eating and I took my ass upstairs, so I could go to sleep. I can't wait to wake up to get the fuck out of here.

~

"BITCH, you got a nigga in my muthafuckin' house! In my muthafuckin' bed! You done lost yo' muthafuckin' mind!" Reggie roared.

"Wait, baby, listen. Just let me explain," my momma begged.

I checked the time and it was almost midnight. I'd been sleep for a few hours. Here we go with this shit. I jumped up, wiping my eyes, and making my way out of my room. I'm so sick of this shit, my heart was beating so fast like it was about to jump out my chest. Reggie and my momma were still going back and forth and as I made my way down the hall to their bedroom. I heard a gunshot that caused me to stop in my tracks. I feel like my muthafuckin' heart stopped beating. *Did this nigga just shoot my momma?*

"Reggie... Reggie, please just listen," my momma cried.

I sighed, relieved to hear momma's voice as I made my way to their room.

"You dirty bitch, you got me fucked up! This is the last time you are going to fuck me over!" Pop! As I ran into the room, Reggie shot my mother in the head and her blood spattered all over the headboard. The look on Reggie's face, he couldn't believe that he did what he's done.

"She made me do it. I didn't mean to do it," Reggie struggled to say, slurring his words.

Looking at my beautiful mother stretched out on the bed fucked me up. Even though her light brown eyes were staring at me, I knew she was gone. It's Reggie's fault he made her do the shit that she been doing. With tears in my eyes and memories of my mother from when I was younger coming to mind, in slow motion, I made my way over to the bed. Rubbing my hand over her cheek, it hit me hard. If I thought that it wasn't real it hit me hard that she is really gone and not coming back.

"Get up, Carmen. Get up. Wake up, baby," Reggie whined, shaking my mom.

Looking at this muthafucka after all he has put us through, all the shit that he has done to my mom, all I saw is red. "Bitch ass nigga! You killed her!" I spat.

Before I knew it, I was on his ass. With each punch that I gave to Reggie, I thought about every tear my mom shed for all the years that she lived in hell being married to him. With these parents, I saw and heard shit that I never should have, and that shit changed me. Muthafuckas always hollering how bad I am. *'Damn, he crazy.'* But nobody ever gave a fuck why I am the way am.

I was trying to slam Reggie, but even with him being drunk, he still had height and weight on me, so he didn't fall like I wanted him to. Hitting him, causing him to fall into the nightstand and lose his balance gave me an advantage over him, and he finally fell smacked the ground hard, causing a loud thump to echo throughout the room.

The body shots I was giving him, he was eating and struggling to stay on his feet. His drunk ass flipped me over and as we continued to fight. He dropped his pole and it flew across the hardwood floors. Trying to get Reggie off of me, this shit isn't working. This nigga won't budge. He found some fucking strength and just kept giving me body shots. I started pulling the cord to the lamp, trying to get it to the floor, so I could hit his bitch ass over the head to get him off me.

Pop! Pop! Pop!

More gun shots rang out. Reggie stopped swinging and his blood splattered all over my face. The blood was leaking from his body so fast that my white shirt was red. I pushed him off of me and Ricardo was standing over me with the gun still in his hand, staring at Reggie's body. Looking over at my momma's lifeless body, I ran my hands across my face. Turning to my little brother, I snatched the pole out of his hand and hugged him as tears continued to fall from his eyes.

Ricardo snatched away and ran over to my mom, holding her and talking to her, like she could hear him. Then he started shaking her and trying to wake her up. Him and my momma were close as hell and seeing how he was taking it, I had to look away. I can't see my little brother like this. After a few minutes passed, I had to think of a plan and quick as my brother just continued to cry. Not being able to think of something to fix this shit is fucking with me. I can't believe this shit is happening. *Why my momma? God, can you just bring her back?*

Lost in my thoughts, I didn't even know how the fuck to feel. My momma was gone and no matter how much I prayed or shook her, she ain't coming back. I could hear my momma talking to me.

"*Y'all all the fuck y'all got. Never let nothing or nobody ever come in between y'all,"* she would tell me every time we left the house. Through all the shit that we went through, I thought that things couldn't get any worse, but now I know it could.

"Look, Ricardo! I got you. Don't I always have yo muthafucking back?"

"Scar, I'm going to jail. I just killed dad."

"Go in your room. We don't have a lot of time. You know Susie nosy ass done called the fuckin' police and they coming. Go in your room and I don't give a fuck what happens, do not come out!"

With tears still falling down his face, Ricardo hugged me again and made his way out of the room. I grabbed a towel to wipe his fingerprints off the pole. I don't know what the fuck is about to happen, but I do know one thing, they not takin' my muthafuckin' brother. They can take me, and I'll be back to get my brother.

3

SCAR

3 Years Later...

"My baby!" Pumpkin screamed as the guard walked me to meet her and client manager, Susan Combs.

"What's up, Pumpkin," I said as Pumpkin wrapped her arms around me and hugged me tight as hell.

"I need you sign these papers and then you can go. I need you to understand that even though you are being released, you are going to remain under supervision. Everything that we discussed, you need to understand that one time fucking up, and you'll be going to the Colorado Department of Corrections," Susan spat.

"Pumpkin, let me sign these papers, so we can get the fuck out of here," I said. Pumpkin was still squeezing me tight like she does every time she sees me.

Pumpkin hesitated, but I know she can tell by the way I was mugging this bitch, we needed to get the fuck out of here. Pumpkin let me go and didn't budge from my side. Susan looked me and Pumpkin up and down like we are beneath her and she's more than what her bitch ass is. I hate this bitch. No good luck and well wishes. All this bitch do is threaten to lock me back the fuck up. I ain't even out of the fucking door yet!

Pumpkin is my muthafuckin' dawg. She's my mom's twin sister. Her and my momma were best friends, so losing my mom hit her hard. She blames herself for not knowing what was going on at our house, but that shit wasn't her fault. Looking at Pumpkin always makes a nigga feel a way because she looks just like my momma. Her mouth is smart just like her, but Pumpkin won't just talk shit, she'll get it poppin'.

Ma was one of the people that drilled *what goes on in this house, stays in this house*. My momma never told Pumpkin what Reggie was doing, and we damn sure never told her. Me and Ricardo spent a lot of time at Pumpkin's house when we were younger, but the older we got, the less we saw her until all that shit went down. The thing is, when we needed her Pumpkin didn't hesitate and she came thru.

If it wasn't for Pumpkin, I don't know how the fuck I would have made it through this shit. She has always been solid and no matter what, she is always down with me and my brother. When they offered me a deal, I took it. I didn't end up having to do the whole thing, which would have been five years. Pumpkin didn't want me to take the deal, she wanted me to fight the case, but they could have given me way more time even considering the situation.

My lawyer, not being sure that he could bring me home, is what made me make my decision to take the plea. He wanted Ricardo to testify, but I can remember my momma telling me that I had to protect my little brother no matter what. Bringing him into the courtroom to make him relive the bullshit that we went through, I would never do that. Pumpkin stepping up and looking out for R'Shad while I was gone meant everything to a nigga. For that, she will always be my heart.

"You need to be at my office tomorrow at nine' o clock. If you are a minute late, I'll be issuing a warrant for your arrest," Susan said, handing me a copy of the terms of my parole.

I didn't even waste my time responding. I walked away, leaving her ass standing there. I know what the fuck I have to do. I'm just ready to get this shit done. I just want to get to it, so I don't have to look at that bitch no longer than I got to. Pumpkin walked right behind me. She's happier than I am that I'm finally free.

To be honest, shit, it doesn't seem real. Looking back over my shoulder, I'm just waiting for them muthafuckas to come out and tell me that it was a mistake and I'm not going home. Being locked up and away from my family wasn't some shit that was easy for a nigga and that time that I missed, I can never get back. What fucks with me the most is that I couldn't go to my momma's funeral. I just wanted to see her one last time and apologize for not protecting her. They wouldn't even let me do that, even with the proof that my lawyer presented about Reggie and his long as criminal history.

"It's finally here, baby, and you coming home!" Pumpkin screamed as she hugged me again tightly.

"Damn, Pumpkin, how many times are you gon' to hug me?" I said as Pumpkin stopped squeezing me.

"Nigga, as many times as I want to. I'm so happy that yo' rude ass is home. If I was that bitch, Felicia, ya black ass wouldn't care how many times I hugged you," Pumpkin spat, lighting up a cigarette as we got in her car.

"Did she call you? Where the fuck she at?" I asked.

"Yea, she been calling my damn house too damn much. I don't like that bitch. I know that you think you in love and shit, but watch her," Pumpkin said, taking her eyes off the road, looking me in the eyes.

"Pumpkin, you don't like nobody. Fe been down with a nigga through all this shit. All these years and you still won't give her a chance? She ain't been out here fucking with none of the bum ass niggas. Whenever I called, she answered, and I never had to question her about shit," I said, causing Pumpkin to roll her eyes.

"You heard what I said. Watch that sticky fingers little bitch. I check that hoe's pockets every time she leaves my house."

"She would never take nothing from you, P. Where my brother at?"

"I don't want to hear that shit. If a muthafucka will steal from anybody, my black ass ain't exempt. That bitch will rob me blind too shit! But Ricardo at the house with Cina."

"You fuck with Cina, I see?" I said because I been peeped that every time I call P, Cina is over there.

"She's cool, and her ass can cook. She always at my damn house, but Ricardo wants her there. And if it keeps him out the street a little, shit, I'll put up with her."

Leaning back in my seat, I thought about all the shit that I had to do. Pumpkin has all these plans, but I don't know about the shit she's talking about. As long as I don't get caught up in no bullshit, I can get off parole early and be done with this shit, which is what the fuck I'm trying to do. The quicker I can get done with this shit, the better because Susan stay on some bullshit. She can't wait to lock a muthafucka back up whether they deserve it or not.

"Here, this damn girl already texting and calling my phone," Pumpkin said, handing me her phone.

I knew from looking at the phone that it's Fe. "Why you ain't got her number saved?" I asked.

"She's yo' bitch, not mine. Why the fuck do I need to save her number? Ricardo got you a phone, it's at the house. I don't want that bitch keep blowing up my damn phone," Pumpkin said as she jumped on the highway.

4

RICARDO

"Cina, what's wrong?" I asked. I could tell by the look on her face that she had an attitude about something.

"Nothing. Same ol' shit, my momma. I don't want to be there no more, Chaos," Cina whined.

"I know, Cee. I'm trying to get shit together, so I can get you out of there. It's too many muthafuckas in this house and my brother coming home today."

"I don't want to put all that on you. I know what yo' plan is and what you tryin' to do. It's not yo' job to get me out of Rita's house."

I just looked at her and made my way upstairs. We'd been having this conversation for the past month. I love Cina. I'll do anything for her, and she knows that. If I say something, I mean it. I'm not the type of nigga to try to gas her. I was trying to leave the streets alone and just focus on school and shit because Pumpkin been on my ass about school. I just got off of probation for possession and assault charges. A few days after I finished probation,

I caught new charges. Right now, I got to do what the fuck I got to.

I hate having to have the same conversation with Cee over and over about the same shit. Her momma doesn't like me, and I don't like that bitch either. I never did anything to her or Cee. She ain't got no real reason, but she always starting shit with Cee about me. Rita is just a mad, bitter ass bitch and that's all that it is. Cee is always over here. She hardly even goes to that bitch's house, but whenever she does, it's always some bullshit when she comes back.

Emptying my pockets, I put all the money I made today in my stash in my closet. Plopping down on my bed, I thought of all the ways I could make some shit shake and make sure that Cina is good. I don't give a fuck about Rita, but seeing the way that it fucks with her, it's been making a nigga want to cut ties and let her go on about her life. I love Cina, but maybe she needs to be with a nigga that's getting some real money and can give her all the shit she wants and deserves. Maybe I need to just walk away and come back for her when I can make shit right. It's fuckin' with me, it mkes me feel like a bitch ass nigga for not being able to make sure that Cina is good.

I heard Cina coming up the stairs. Checking the time on my phone, P and R'Shad should be here soon. Looking over at Cee, I could tell she'd been downstairs crying. Her makeup was all fucked up and her eyes were puffy and shit.

"Cee, come here," I said, waving her over.

"I know you sick of hearing about Rita. I don't want you to feel like you have to keep hustlin' for me. I know you want to leave the streets alone," Cina said as she sat in my lap and wet up my T- Shirt with more tears falling from her eyes.

"Cee, I told you I would handle it and I meant that. This shit is for us, and as long as you stay by my side, I promise I'll always make sure that we're good. Quit going over there. Fuck Rita. You don't have to go back over there. You can stay here until I put some shit together," I said, even though I wasn't sure if it's what we both need.

"Pumpkin doesn't want me here."

"I got you, Cee."

"You not alone in this, Chaos. We can do this together, and I've been telling you that. I've been saving the money I been making from doing nails and lashes."

I didn't respond to Cina, I just kissed her thick lips. Cina is the baddest female out here. Ain't none of these bitches fucking with her. She's chocolate with beautiful, clear skin, dark brown eyes and long black hair that touches her waist. Cina is thick as fuck with perfect titties, thick thighs, wide hips and a fat, juicy ass that sits up just right. Every nigga wants her, but she's loyal and none of them niggas can't even get close to her.

"Go get yo'self together. We'll talk about this later. I need to go make sure shit is right for when Scar gets here," I said as Cina kissed me and jumped up and made her way to the bathroom.

Being 17, my only concern should be figuring out what college I'm going to and what Jordan's come out on Saturday. But ever since that my momma got killed, I had to grow up, fast. Pumpkin took me in even when all of our other family told her to let me into the system, foster care or some shit. They told her to cut ties with

Scar, but she didn't. Being the reason Scar was locked up really fucks with me. It's some shit I think about every day.

I wanted to tell everybody that I'm the one who shot and killed Reggie, but Scar wouldn't let me. Every time I went to see him and brought up what happened, he cut me off and wouldn't even speak on it. We never even told Pumpkin what really happened. My momma always told me to watch Scar, but even though he stayed in some shit, he made sure that I was good. Scar was always there for me and when they took my nigga away, I didn't know how the fuck I was going to make it.

When I moved in with Pumpkin and my cousin, Antonio, he introduced me the streets. Scar used to hustle the niggas at the park shooting dice, but never anything more than that. The money me and my cousin been getting is cool, but I know that it can be better. Antonio be on bullshit doe. With my brother coming home today, I know we can make some big shit happen.

"You excited about Scar coming home?" Cee yelled from the bathroom.

"Yea, I missed my nigga! With him being home, shit really about to get good!"

"Chaos, get this hot ass car the fuck up the street and away from my damn house!" Pumpkin yelled from downstairs.

I didn't waste my time responding. I just made my way downstairs to see my brother. Pumpkin only calls me Chaos when she's mad. I meant to move my G-whip before they made it here, but I forgot. I stole it from the airport three days ago. It's about time to get rid of it anyways and get something else. I could have bought an ol' school or some shit, but I'm saving my money for some more important shit.

"Damn, Lil nigga! Yo' lil ass done finally started growing!" Scar yelled, looking me up and down.

"Fuck you, nigga! I ain't no lil nigga no more!" I spat as we both busted out laughing.

It felt good that Scar was finally home. Hugging my nigga, we both just kept looking at each other, taking it all in. The years that we have been apart haven't been easy, and I blamed myself for all the time that he missed out here when it should have me sitting down doing the time. Scar was always there to make sure I was good. Nobody wouldn't even think about pressing me because they didn't want it with him. Even the OG's on the block, they respected Scar because won't no hoe in his blood, and there wasn't a nigga walking that he would let hoe him.

"This is my girl, Cina," I said as Cina came into the living room.

"Hi. Chaos talks about you all the time, it's nice to meet you," Cina said as she grabbed my arm.

"Not as much as he talks about you. You got this nigga sprung. When I left, this nigga was scared to talk to bitches, now he in love," Scar said, laughing hard as hell. Pumpkin joined in to.

"Fuck y'all," I said, hugging and kissing Cee on the cheek.

"I'll let you spend some time with yo' brother. I'm going to go and meet Sameria. I'll be back," Cee said as she broke our embrace.

"We know you'll be back, girl. You need to start paying rent over here," Pumpkin said as I walked Cee outside.

"You don't have to leave, Cina," I said once we made it to the porch.

"I know, I'll be back later. I know how much yo' brother means to you. Y'all been separated for a long-time, baby. I'll be back."

"Don't go to Rita's," I said, meaning that shit.

"Alright."

"I'm not playing, Cina."

5

CINA MILLER

I made my way down the street to my bestie's house. I just kept thinking about what Chaos said about not going back to Rita's. It's one thing to cut ties with Rita, but my little brother, Sincere, is who I'm worried about. Well, him and the fact that I'm trying to protect Chaos. The only person that I trust to open up and tell everything to is Sameria, my best friend, so that's where I'm going.

"Rita, just called over here looking for you," Sameria said as she swung the door open.

I acted like I didn't hear her and made my way into the house. Looking around, I saw her momma was gone. I plopped down on the couch relieved because I got my own damn problems. I don't want to hear her mouth today. Sameria went right back to cleaning like I wasn't even here. Every time I come over here, she be cleaning like she's the damn maid. I don't know whose situation is worse, hers or mine.

"What you doing over here? Where is Chaos at?"

"You know Rita still on that bullshit, so I just go to

check on Sin and then get the fuck on. I'm sick of her shit. I'm not gon' be able to take too much more of being under her roof. Chaos is at Pumpkin's. His brother just got out, so I'm letting him spend time with him. We 'bout to get fucked up tonight doe, are you coming?" I said as I jumped up to help Sameria finish cleaning because she's sneaking out this bitch tonight.

"Girl, I can't wait to leave for school. I'm so sick of Susie and her shit. I'm supposed to take care of Tasia while she's at work day and night. She treats me like a fucking slave."

"What about Rodney? How does he feel about you leaving town?"

"I love him, Cee. Rodney is still on some bullshit and I haven't heard from him in three days. I been blowing up his phone and I even popped up at his house since he been skipping school. I'm not about to keep chasing him. All he wants to do is run the streets and party. He doesn't understand that I can't do that every night."

"You need to leave Rodney alone. Fuck him! It's too many niggas out here to be trippin' over a nigga that ain't shit and ain't gon' to be ever be shit. He thinks 'cause he getting money, he can do as he pleases since all these bitches throwin' they pussy at him left and right. I don't want you to leave. Why can't you just go to the University of Denver or Metro?" I asked as it started to sink in that before I know it, Sameria is going to be leaving for college.

"I'm going to miss yo' ass too, but bitch, I'm not staying here. You'll be good, ain't shit gon' change between us. We'll still talk every day and bitch, you better not be trying to make no new friends. I fight bitches over my bestie. Plus, you got Chaos. Bitch, you always with that nigga. With Scar getting out, you better be careful. You know they say that nigga crazy."

"You know I don't fuck with nobody but you and Unique. That ain't gon' change. I don't do bitches. But yo' friendly ass better not move to Texas and make no new friends, hoe!"

I made my way to the kitchen to make some dish water, so we can get this shit over and hit the mall to get something to wear for tonight. Meria and me finished catching up with everything that happened since we saw each other in school. Every time I hear the bullshit that nigga Rodney be on, I just want to find that hoe ass nigga and jump out on him. He does the most and he not even that nigga.

I know she says that she loves him, but I think she just blinded by the shit he does for her. That nigga stays on bullshit, and he's been able to get away with it because he keeps her purse full and whatever she wants she gets. In return, he fuckin' on whoever, wherever. I know that her situation is fucked up with her momma, but she is the smartest person that I know. She gets all A's and has been accepted to several colleges. She is graduating a year early at only 16 because she so damn smart.

Cina is not just smart, my bitch is bad as fuck. She has pretty yellow skin, pretty big, brown eyes and long, black hair that hits the middle of her back and it's all hers, no bundles.. She has a small waist, thick thighs and lil bootie. Niggas always are trying to shoot their shot, but she's loyal to the soil and as long as she's with her nigga she's going to ride 'til the fucking end.

We are the total opposite. While I want to party and

kick it, Meria would much rather be in the house reading. The only time I can get her out is when she fed up with her nigga, momma or both. Meria wants to be a nurse and I know she's going to make it through nursing school with no problem. Then there's me. I skip my first two classes every day and finally wake up and make my way to class when Pumpkin starts cussing my ass out. Meria has never missed one class and no matter how much I beg; her ass won't ever skip with me. I'll be sixteen next month, and I'm a Sophomore and I hate school and can't wait for it to be over.

Even though me and Meria are different, our bond could never be fucked with. If we could have been born into different families, maybe our lives could be different. Her momma expects her to raise her little sister. She has to make sure she Tasia eats, wash her clothes, get her to and from school and every damn thing else. That's her daughter, not her sister. Susie gets on my damn nerves. I don't see how Meria deals with her, but I guess we're just doing what we have to do. And that is the only reason why I deal with Rita.

"I'm surprised to see you over here. I been seeing yo' fast ass running behind that that lil yellow boy," Susie said from behind me as she came through the back door.

"Hey, Ma," I said and turned around, rolling my eyes while finishing up the dishes.

I'm fast for being with one nigga and only one nigga. The only nigga that I've ever been with and the only one I'm ever going to be with. Susie is my God mom. Her and my mom used to be tight like me and Meria, but now they won't even speak to each other. She thinks that everybody should just sit in the house all the time and be like Meria. After I finished washing the dishes, I made sure the rest of the kitchen was good and took out the trash. This is nothing new. every time I'm over here, I help Meria, so she can leave the house.

"Where you think you goin'?" Susie asked with an attitude.

I made my way to the living room, to get my purse and phone. That's my sign to get the fuck on. She can meet me around the corner at Rita's. I need to go and check on Sincere. "Well, if you goin' to library, you takin', Tasia with you, and make sure my baby hair is looking decent. Don't take her out this house looking a mess. Make sure she eat and her homework is done. I have to be to work in a few hours." I heard Susie say as I closed the bathroom door behind me.

I kept going to the bathroom to check and see if my period started. I was three weeks late and starting to get worried. Chaos could get my hair and nails done and buy me Jordan's, but taking care of a baby isn't something he can do right now. I used the bathroom and just like I already knew before I came in here, my period still hasn't come. I got myself together and made my way out the bathroom.

I was trying to get my money up, so me and Chaos can do this shit together. I have always loved doing nails. I started out just doing mine and my girls. Bitches stay trying to play with me with my prices because I'm not licensed yet. I know my shit is good and even better than the shit bitches pay shops for. My text messages and dm's stay poppin' with bitches trying to get in. Pumpkin stays talking shit, but she been letting me do nails and lashes in the empty room at her house. I knew that Scar was coming home, and I was going to have to find somewhere for my clients to come to. I hate feeling like I'm stressing Chaos out with my problems. Shit, I know he got his own shit going on. I'm going to let him enjoy tonight with his brother, but tomorrow we are going to have to sit down and come up with a plan.

I snatched up my juice and Meria was tightening up Tasia's pony tails.

"Meria! That hurts! Don't do it so tight!" Tasia whined.

"Girl, sit still. Stop moving before I pop you with this brush. Girl let me get us together then I'll meet you at Rita's. Did you take it?" Meria asked, catching me off guard.

"No," I said as I started fumbling with my fingernails.

"Bitch, I don't know what you waiting for. You need to take it. Bitch, what the fuck I got to do, sit in the bathroom with you and hold yo' fucking hand?"

"I'm going to take it," I said, referring to the pregnancy test I bought earlier.

"Bitch, hurry up. I'm 'bout to be in and out of my mommas," I said and made my way out the front door.

My momma makes sure my little brother is good. She'll do anything for him. It's not a secret that Sincere is her favorite. She doesn't hesitate to remind me every time I see her. Rita hates me because my dad left her when I was five years old. How he left and how he treats her now is the reason why she treats me the way that she does. You would think it would have brought us closer, but that ain't how shit worked out for us.

It's not like he left her, but still was there for me. Shit, I haven't seen him since he left. I haven't gotten a birthday card, Christmas present, not even a phone call in all the years that he has been gone. I'm not mad. Shit, I don't even trip on it anymore. Rita is miserable enough for the both of us. My dad's sister, Faith, always looks out for me and she gives Rita money every month, but I never see it.

When I got across the street from my house, I could see my cousin, Lil Miller's car in the driveway. I hesitated, but the way the wind was blowing and hitting my face, I ran across the street. When I got to Meria's, it was nice as fuck out. I was carrying my coat and now it's freezing cold and about to snow. I started fumbling through my purse, looking for my keys.

I knocked on the door 'cause I couldn't find them bitches fast enough. I know everybody's sitting right there in the living room, but nobody even bothered to come to the door. I finally found my keys and ran in the house as fast as I could. When I walked in, the smell of weed and alcohol hit me hard. One thing I can say, Rita makes sure her house is clean at all times, but that's about the only good thing that I can say. I don't have to be a slave and clean up after her and all her company.

"Look who decided to come home. You think that you can just come and go from here as much as you please? Utt unn, bitch, this ain't what you 'bout to keep doing," my momma said as I rubbed my hands together trying to warm up and unzipping my coat.

"What up, cuz?" Lil Miller asked.

I nodded my head and made my way through the house to go and check on Sin. I'm not about to argue with Rita. She let Lil Miller just come over here and do whatever the fuck he wants out of her house. He has his niggas and crackheads running in and out of here and Rita don't give a fuck, but she worried about me not being here. Who the fuck wants to be here?

I went into Sin's room where he was playing the game, not paying me any attention. "Hey, Sin. Did you eat?" I asked as I plopped down on his bed. Sin caught me up with everything that I'd missed the past few days not being here. When I was crying earlier at Chaos's, I know that I told him I was crying about what happened at Rita's, but I was just thinking about how shit is going and how it could get worse with us having a baby.

"Hey, cuz. Let me holla at you for a second," Lil Miller said, standing in Sin's doorway.

I rolled my eyes, got up and followed him down the hall. My cousin is a vulture and that nigga loves preying on anybody. A muthafucka that he can get the inside scoop on is an easy lick for him. This is another reason why I want to stay the fuck away from here. My momma doesn't know the type of money that Chaos is getting, but her and my cousin assume by how he dresses and the car he drives that he's touching way more than he is.

"Look, I know that you love that nigga or whatever, but check this out. The way I can set this shit up, that nigga will never know you had anything to do with it. I got you, we can do this shit one time and the right way then we can both get paid, cuz," Lil Miller said, rubbing his hands together.

"I don't give a fuck what plan you done came up with now, nigga, I'm not doing it. Find another nigga to get," I said. I turned to walk away and was met by Rita blocking me from getting by.

"Look, you lil yellow bitch, you either listen to what the fuck Lil Miller has planned and play yo' muthafuckin' part or yo' ass can go to Pumpkin's and don't worry about comin' back here," Rita spat and blew smoke from her blunt into my face.

"I'll leave," I said, not even hesitating.

"You can leave, but you ain't taking none of the shit in my house with you and don't bring yo' ass nowhere near my muthafuckin' house or my son!" Rita spat in my face, knowing that would hurt me the most.

"Cuz, let's just get this money and then we can all get paid," Lil' Miller said, looking at me up and down, trying to convince me to see things their way.

I just stood there looking at my momma, trying to figure out what I did to deserve her as a mother. Your mother is supposed to be loving, caring, your first teacher and the woman that helps to guide you through life. My momma has never been any of that. The sad thing is she will never be, no matter how many years pass by and how much I pray for things to change. I know that Lil Miller doesn't give a fuck about me or Chaos, but for my momma to be willing to put me in this shit, that shit hurts bad.

"You are taking too damn long to decide. Whose fucking side are you on? You came out of my pussy! Before that nigga showed you a little bit of attention, yes bitch, a little attention because I know that he is fucking on four or five more bitches too, so don't feel special! If you can't do this for all of us, the family, then get the fuck out my house! When that nigga through with yo' ass and get sick of you, don't bring yo' ass back here. Once you leave, ain't no coming back!" Rita spat in between choking on her blunt.

"What's going on, why y'all screamin'?" Sincere asked as he came out of his bedroom.

I brushed past Miller and didn't even waste my time responding to Rita. I went over to my brother and hugged him tight. Him being twelve and my only sibling, we have always been close, so this wasn't going to be easy. I'm not going to let Rita keep me away from Sin, I don't give a fuck what she says. Tears burning my skin, they fell faster than I could wipe.

I know Chaos, and he has his flaws and shit that I don't like. But one things for sure, he's definitely not the type of nigga that would cheat on me. The fucked-up part is that my momma says that shit every time I see her. Tearing me down is some shit that makes her happy and if she doesn't say some hurtful shit to me, it just wouldn't be right.

"What's wrong, Cina? Why you cryin'?" Sin asked.

"I'll be good, I'll see you later," I said, hugging Sin tightly. I turned to walk away with Rita still standing in the same spot, preventing me from getting to the front door.

Knock, Knock, knock.

"That nigga doesn't really want you, bitch. He's just going to play with yo' ass as long as he wants to and then be on to the next bitch. He'll probably get yo' dumb ass pregnant and then leave yo' ass with nothing! You sittin' around Pumpkin's fake ass and you think that means something. That bitch just blowing smoke up yo' ass. Whenever yo' ass ain't there, the next bitch over there having family time, dumb ass!"

"You just mad because Chaos really does love me, and he's not going to leave me! What type of woman would wish bad on their own daughter—" I attempted to say before my momma cut me off, slapping me so hard I fell back into the wall.

"When yo' ass decided to go against the grain, I no longer had a daughter!" Rita screamed.

I caught my balance and pushed past her. Zipping up my coat and putting my hood on my head, I prepared myself for the cold ass air I was about to walk back into. I was met at the front door by Tasia and Meria. Meria knows everything there is to know about me, not to mention this is something that my momma and Lil Miller been plotting on for months, so I didn't even have to tell her why I was crying.

"Don't even think about trying to take yo' ass to my sister house either! You lil ungrateful bitch!" Rita spat, slamming the front door as we made our way to the cab that was waiting for us.

6

SAMERIA

I get so sick of always having to watch Tasia. I know my mom has to work, but damn, who the fuck said I have to be the designated babysitter. Every once in a while, she goes with our grandma, but if she's not with our grandma, she's right by my side. My momma is always at work. I do appreciate everything that she does for me, but I can't wait to be out on my own, so I can live my life and not have to be worried about Tasia all the time.

I always thought things would've been different if my dad was still here. My dad was killed when I was seven years old. When he was around, things were nothing like they are now. I was daddy's little girl and that's something I don't think I will ever get over or my momma. My mom has changed so much since my dad got murdered and I wish that she would go back to the woman she used to be. Me and my momma used to be close. I told her everything and she was like my best friend. Now my mom never has time and went from being a happy, caring person to being angry all the damn time.

I made my way down the hall to check on Tasia one more time. Cracking open her door, I saw her knocked out sleeping. I turned down the volume on her TV and quietly closed her door back. I didn't plan on staying at the party too long because I have to make it home before my momma gets off work. I'd be right across the street and Tasia knows my number by heart. So if she wakes up for some reason, she won't hesitate to blow up my phone until I answer.

I made my way down the hallway to my room. Checking my hair again in the mirror, making sure that it was right, I looked over my outfit for the hundredth time. I was wearing a black and white Nike sweat suit with matching black high-top Airforce one's. Applying more lip gloss and putting on my gold hoops that matched the gold necklace Rodney bought me, I decided I was satisfied with how I looked. I made my way out the house and down the street to Pumpkin's.

"Who is that?" I heard a nigga ask as Pumpkin let me in the house.

"You look cute," Pumpkin said as she lit up a cigarette and hit it hard as hell.

"Thanks, Pumpkin. Where is Cina?" I asked, looking around the room at all the niggas and bitches that came by to welcome Scar home.

"Bonnie got her ass back there in the kitchen," Pumpkin said, laughing.

I could feel Scar staring at me, but I wasn't the only that peeped he was looking too hard. His bitch, Felicia, was pissed and the way he dismissed her ass made her even more pissed. I couldn't help but laugh as I spoke to Antonio's drunk ass. That is one reason why I don't like drinking like that because muthafuckas get to drinking and can't handle they liquor.

"So, you really just gon' to stare at that bitch? Nigga, I'm sitting right here!" Felica screamed so loud, catching everybody's attention.

"Fe, chill the fuck out. What the fuck is you talking 'bout? I'm not thinking about that bitch. You worried about the wrong shit." Scar spat as I made my way through the house.

I couldn't help but laugh. Scar looked like the type of nigga that would fuck with a bitch like Fe. Damn near the whole hood done ran through that bitch, and he just getting his turn. Everything that bitch got on, she hit the mall and took. The hole on the side of her jogging suit just lets me know my suspicions about this scandalous hoe are right because I can see where the ink tag was.

"Bitch, I thought I was gon' to have to come over there and kidnap yo' ass!" Cina yelled over the music as I walked in the kitchen.

"Bitch, whatever. I had to wait until Tasia was sleep before I came over here. I'm not staying all night."

"Here, bitch, drink some of this. Give me' yo coat, so I can go put it up," Cina said as all the niggas shooting dice started talking shit because, like always, Chaos was winning.

Pumpkin was right by calling Cina *Bonnie* because she was right by Chaos's side no matter what. Her family been trying to set up Chaos for minute and Cina never even thought about switching up on Chaos. She gon' to ride with him until the wheels fall off and the best part is he rides for her even harder. He not touching as much money as some other niggas are yet, but it's coming.

"Bitch, I took the test," Cina whispered in my ear.

"Um, bitch, and what the fuck did it say?" I asked, looking at her crazy.

Cina looked at me and mouthed, "I'm pregnant."

I could tell by the look on her face that she was scared and didn't know what she was going to do. "You know I got you, bitch," I said, hugging her and rapping along to the Jeezy song blasting through the house.

I know that Chaos loves my girl by the way he looks at her, touches her and respects her. He will let any and everybody know that Cina's position is held, and he won't even entertain another bitch. Other niggas already know not to even try Cina because although Chaos is quiet and doesn't say much, this nigga will get crazy, and his name fits his ass perfectly. My phone started vibrating, looking down I saw *Maybe: My Baby.*

It took this nigga long enough to return my phone calls. Now all of sudden he wants to talk. It's been days and I haven't heard from him, but as soon as I leave the house here, he comes. I'd be lying if I said I didn't care about Ro. As much as I care about Rodney, I know he's not ever gon' change. I'm tired of waiting for him to change and at this point, I'm just trying to pass time until I leave for college.

"Sameria!" Pumpkin screamed from the other room.

Bobbin' my head, I made my way to find Pumpkin. It felt so damn good to get out of the house, not have to worry about Tasia and just kick it with my girl. This is something that I hardly ever do. Not because I don't want to like everybody just assumes, but because I have to make sure my little sister is good. Getting out the house and not sitting around thinking about Ro, blowing him up while he does whatever the fuck he wants to do... I had to do tonight.

"Yo' nigga is outside. I'm not letting him in my house," Pumpkin whispered in my ear once I made it in the living room.

"What do you want Rodney?" I asked, giving him all the attitude that I've had since, he's been missing.

"Why you ignorin' my phone calls and texts?" Rodney asked and went back to mugging me like he was when I walked on the porch.

"When Rodney a few minutes ago because you haven't been returning my calls or text messages."

"You already know what I'm doing, I don't want to hear that shit. I'm getting this money. The same money that paid for yo' hair, nails and that shit you got on right now. Don't play with me, Sameria."

"That's the fucking problem right there. You think that you can do whatever, buy me something, give me a few dollars and then shit is supposed to be all good, but it's not. You can't buy me, Ro. So, who the fuck is Tay?"

Even though I asked the question because I wanted a fucking answer. I know this nigga well enough to know that he's not going to give me one. All he does is lie and eventually get caught when another muthafucka feels it's their place to tell on him. And that's how I found out he was entertaining Tay. Whether he tells me or not, I'm done with his ass. I knew I was done when he didn't answer my calls or texts. There once was a time when I'd put everything on hold just to come running to this nigga but shit ain't the same.

"I don't know what you talkin' 'bout!" Ro spat. As he

began to move around, a breeze came through and Tay walked up on the porch.

"What's up, baby. Why you ain't tell me you were gon' be here?" Tay said like I wasn't standing right here.

"So, you don't know what I'm talkin' 'bout, but this bitch feels comfortable enough to call you *baby*, right?" I yelled, losing my patience.

"Who the fuck you callin' a bitch?" Tay said, turning to me, finally acknowledging that I was even on the porch with them.

Not even wasting my time responding, I pushed Tay's disrespectful ass, causing her to fall into the wall, lose her balance and smack the ground with a loud thump. Wasting no time, I jumped on that bitch. Each time my fist connected to her face, her screams and cries got louder. I pinned her arms down with my knees and kept beating the fuck out of her.

"Alright, that's enough, get up!" Ro spat.

"What the fuck is going on out here? Cina, come and get yo' muthafuckin' friend! My muthafuckin' front porch is not a boxing ring, bitch! Get the fuck up!" I heard Pumpkin scream as she tried to pull me off Tay.

Pumpkin tried to pull me off while Ro's punk ass just stood there and watched, every now and then asking me to stop. He didn't really care 'cause if he did, he would have put this bitch in her place and let it be known what the fuck it was, but he didn't. I don't give a fuck what he says or buys after this shit, I'm done with him.

"Y'all got to get the fuck out of here with all this bull-shit!" I heard a nigga scream from behind me, causing me to jump.

As I went to bang Tay's head into the ground, I was swooped up off the ground. "Let go of her muthafuckin' hair!" Turning around, still gripping Tay's hair, I saw it was Scar. I don't fight often, but when I do, I'm not stopping until my point has been made

"If you hit me, I promise you I'm gon' fuck you up!" Scar spat.

"Nigga, put my bitch down! Sameria, come the fuck on. Let's get the fuck out of here," Ro said like he was irritated by me fighting one of his bitches.

"I don't know who the fuck you think you talkin' to ! I'm not one of these bitches, you bitch ass nigga, but we can take this shit outside!" Scar barked, putting me on my feet.

"Nigga, we'll see each other soon. I got to get to this money. Sameria, get to the fucking car!" Ro spat, mugging me and Scar.

"Fuck you! I'm not going nowhere with you! Nigga, are you crazy? Take that bitch with you too!" I spat, kicking Tay off the porch and into the snow covering the ground at least a good five inches.

"You gon' choose these muthafuckas over me? After all the shit I've done for you! Fu—" Ro attempted to say, but Scar hit him so hard, he fell into the screen door, knocking it off the hinges, falling into the snow with his bitch.

"Get in the house now, R'Shad!" Pumpkin screamed so loud, her voice cracked.

"Bitch, what you doin' fighting bitches and shit?" Cina asked while ushering me in the house.

I just want to get my coat and go home. I know that

everybody that knows me and Rodney are together just assume I'm dumb and he is never going to change. I do love him, and I used to be able to say that he was loyal and not doing me wrong, but that is no longer the case. Every time I turn around, this nigga is doing me wrong. I'm supposed to just sit back, not say shit and he can keep doing whatever the fuck he wants to do.

Cina ushered me upstairs to Chaos's room. She'd been telling me to leave Ro alone, so I already know what she's going to say. I should have listened to her months ago when I heard about the last bitch he was fucking with. I'm not tripping on Tay because she don't owe me shit, my nigga did.

"Meria, I know that you have feelings for Rodney, but you need to let that nigga go! For real, fuck him! It's a nigga out here that will love and respect you, you don't have to accept that bullshit from him. Bitch, do you know how many niggas would love to have a bitch like you?" Cina said as I let the tears that I was holding back fall.

Cina hugged me tight. "Meria, you gon' be good. I got you. If you wana go and bust all the windows out that nigga's car and flatten all his tires, we can do that too, bitch! Whatever you want to do, I'm ready, just let me know!" Cina screamed, causing me to laugh.

Pop! Pop! Pop! Rat-a-tat-a-tat-a-tatat!

The sound of bullets flying through the house and screams were all that could be heard. Cina and I both hit the floor. She prayed out loud, asking God to protect her baby and Chaos. We both screamed as we crawled under the bed and the sound of the gunfire just kept ringing in my ear. Just when I thought the shooting was over, it seemed like more bullets kept coming. I just kept praying, asking God to make it stop.

"Cina! Cee!" Chaos called out from a distance.

"I'm good, I'm not coming out!" Cina replied in between crying.

"Arrgggh, fuck!" I heard someone scream out in pain.

Cina and I were hugging each other as we both cried. After what seemed like forever, the gunfire stopped, but my ears are still ringing. I could hear several people screaming and somebody crying as Cina and I looked at eachother with tears and fear in both of our eyes. It was written all over Cina's face. I waited for Cina to take the lead and tell me it's okay for us to come from under the bed.

"Cina! Cee, baby. Help me," Chaos grunted.

Cina rushed from under the bed, not thinking twice about it. I followed right behind her. I needed to get the fuck out of here and go home before the police get here and call my momma. It's always something and this is another reason why I stay my ass at home. We can't ever just have a good time and kick it; niggas have to shoot shit up.

Cina rushed to Chaos's side. Walking into the hallway, he was sprawled out on the floor with blood leaking from his side. "Move out my way! R'Shad, call a fucking ambulance! They shot my baby!" Pumpkin screamed, running up the stairs, damn near knocking me over and pushing Cina to be by Chaos's side.

After a few minutes passed, the police and EMT's came rushing into the house and damn near flew up the stairs. Helping Cina up off the floor, I held her as she cried. Looking at Chaos bleed out is something that I will probably never forget. Hearing Cina and Pumpkin cry out for help caused my heart to ache. I know how much Cina loves Chaos and the fact that she is carrying his child, I can only imagine all the things that were going through her mind.

7

CINA

"Ma'am, I'ma need to talk to you two," an officer said to me and Sameria, following the EMT's down the stairs as they rushed Chaos out the house.

"I'm not fuckin' talkin' to you about shit! Do you see my boyfriend?" I screamed at twelve and ran out the house.

"Only one of you can ride with him," one of the EMT's said with an attitude.

Meria hugged me. "Call me and let me know what's going on, Cee. I love you."

I jumped in the back of the ambulance with Chaos as the EMT's proceeded to work on him, trying to keep up on everything they were saying and making sure that I didn't miss anything. I couldn't help but think about Lil Miller and how he could possibly have something to do with this. To somebody with regular parents, they might not be able to even imagine their family shooting up a house knowing they're in it. But with my family, that's the type of shit they do. Every time the ambulance made a sharp turn, I felt like I was about to be sick.

My phone started ringing in my pocket. Looking at the caller id, I saw it was Rita calling. As we pulled up to University Hospital, my anxiety started to get worse. I just let Rita go to the voicemail, I can't deal with her right now. One of the EMT's tried to calm me down while ensuring me that everything is going to be okay and Chaos is going to pull through. As if we didn't have other shit we needed to be worried about, now this.

When I got back from the mall, I took the pregnancy test. Continuing to put it off wasn't going to change the results. Just like I figured, I was pregnant, but I wasn't even able to tell Chaos. I planned to tell him once every-thing calmed down and the party was over. Now the thought of never being able to tell him caused me to be sick to my stomach. What if he isn't here for our child? How am I going to do this shit by myself? Why is this happening? Shit can never go right for me.

As they got Chaos out of the ambulance, my phone started ringing again but this time it was Pumpkin. Following close behind the stretcher, I took a deep breath and answered her call. As I tried to follow Chaos and the EMT's to the back, I was stopped in my tracks by a nurse. She didn't hesitate to let me know I couldn't go with him. She ushered me to the lobby then told me to wait and someone would be out soon to talk to me.

"What's going on? How is my baby?" Pumpkin blurted out as I answered the call.

"I don't know anything yet, we just got to the hospital. They're making me wait in the lobby," I said, pacing the floor.

"Muthafucka, you need to be taking pictures of shell casings and measuring holes in my fucking walls! Not looking through my fucking drawers, muthafucka!" Pumpkin yelled into my ear as Rita beeped in on my other line.

"I'll call you when I find out anything," I said as Pumpkin continued screaming and cussing out the police.

"All this because of yo' fucking friend's punk ass boyfriend!" Pumpkin spat and hung up on me.

I made my way over to the desk to see if they could give me an update on Ricardo. I'm about to get on these people's fucking nerves and I don't care. I'm about to be asking for an update every five minutes until I'm in the back by his side. The woman told me to give her a few minutes and she would go and check on his status. I didn't respond. I walked away so she could go check.

"What do you want, Rita? Why the fuck do you keep calling me?" I asked as I answered the phone.

"Damn, you ain't dead," Rita said, sounding defeated.

I didn't even respond to her hateful ass. I just hung up on her and blocked her number. I feel like everybody in the emergency room's eyes were on me. I can't help it I don't know what to think all I keep thinking about is all the fucked up out comes. No matter how hard I try I can't imagine Chaos walking out of here and being okay. With the way my life has been lately, I just can't imagine things ending well.

"Come on, Cina, you need to sit down." I heard a voice say from behind me.

Turning around, Meria wrapped her arms around me. It felt so good to see her. I figured that she was going home because if her momma finds out that she ain't in that house, she will never hear the end of it.

"Bitch, you knew I wasn't going to leave you up here by yo'self. Come on, let's sit down," Meria said, ushering me over to a chair.

"Meria, this is all my fault. I know Lil Miller did this shit. What the fuck am I going to do if Chaos doesn't pull through? How am I going to explain this to Pumpkin and Scar? What about my baby? Meria, how am I going to explain to my child that my snake ass family killed their dad?" I whined as tears started to fall fast and Meria hugged me tight.

"Cina, this is not your fault. I have to tell you something," Meria said as she rubbed my back.

"What?" I asked in-between wiping my eyes.

"I don't know if it was for sure Miller that did this," Meria said, biting her lip.

"Bitch, I was so scared that something happened to you. Aunt Rita called my momma saying that Chaos's house got shot up!" My loud ass cousin Unique said like she wasn't standing right by me as I looked up.

"Girl, I'm good. Why are you so damn loud?" I spat, taking my attitude out on her as she wrapped her arms around me.

I don't care about Unique being here. I want to know what Sameria was going to say before Unique got here. She's not going to say anything that she doesn't want repeated in front of Unique. By the look in her eyes, I can tell something is bothering her, but now I'm going to have to wait for answers.

"I know yo' momma didn't let you come up here to

check on me," I said as I started tapping my foot, trying to stay calm after the nurse gave us an update.

"She do be fuckin' trippin'. I can't even come to Aunt Rita's and leave from there like I had been doing because yo' ass ain't never at home. And you know Rita be on the phone telling her sister everything," Unique said.

I just shook my head. Unique and I were so close that she has a whole section in my closet at Rita's and her own dresser in my room. We were always together. It wasn't much that we didn't do together until I got with Chaos. Unique was talking to Antonio, but when that didn't work out, she stopped coming around as much. I caught Unique up with what happened and what's been going on since the last time we talked. I didn't have to tell her about the bullshit with my momma because in my family, when something happens, it doesn't take long before everybody knows, even if they don't know the real story. Unique already knows how my momma is, so she wasn't surprised. Unique and Meria are cool, but they're not as close as I am to either one of them.

Having Unique and Meria here was helping because if they weren't, I don't know what I'd do. They are the only friends that I have. I don't trust a lot of people, but I know that no matter what I'm going through, they both will always have my back through it all.

"Bitch, are you pregnant?" Unique asked, catching me off guard.

"Why you ask that?"

"Damn, bitch, really? You gon' do me like that? I tell yo' ass every fucking thing. I asked because my momma asked me. With the way she came at me, it sounded like she already knew, but just wanted to see what I was going to say," Unique said, rolling her eyes like I left her out.

"Bitch, chill. I just found out. I haven't told anybody except Meria. I haven't even told Chaos yet. Between my momma and yo' nosy ass momma, they don't need to worry about me because I'm cutting ties with everybody except you and Sincere. Fuck everybody else, I'm done."

"You sure that's a good idea?" Meria asked.

"Yes, I'm sure. I know that Chaos is going to bounce back and be good. I can see the ambition in him. With that and his hustle, he's about to come up. Me, him and our baby are going to be good, believe that. And if anybody doesn't agree with that or isn't supporting my decision, I don't need them in my life. I don't give a fuck who has to go! Chaos has given me nothing but his love and loyalty from the beginning and I'm going to continue to give him mine!"

Even though, I said all that I can't say that I believe it because good things really never happen for me. I can't remember the last time I had a day when I didn't cry. The fucked up thing is when my days are going good it's always somebody in my family that comes a long and fucks things up. There is a chance of things changing, but to be honest my hopes aren't too high. Meria knows me well enough to know that I'm just saying what they want to hear, but Unique is buying it.

HOURS PASSED and finally they were able to get Chaos stable. Sitting by his bedside, holding his hand is all that I have been doing while thanking God for getting him through this. Pumpkin was stretched out on the couch on the other side of the room. I don't want to even close my eyes because I'm scared that I'm going to miss something.

"Bitch, it's almost three o' clock in the morning. I have to get home," Meria said.

"Alright, call me when you get home," I said as Meria bent down to hug me.

I don't know who the fuck shot up Pumpkin's. My momma calling with the shit she said had me feeling like it was definitely Lil Miller. The only thing is, if they killed Chaos, there is no way they could get anything. Then Meria thinking that is was Ro has me second guessing what really happened. To be honest, I just feel like Ro doesn't have it in him to do anything but talk some shit.

8
SCAR

Knock, Knock, Knock.

"Who the fuck is knocking on the door this early?" I spat, rolling over and checking the time.

I was the only one here, so I had to go answer the fucking door. I just got in the bed. After all the bullshit that happened last night, I just want to get a few more hours of sleep before I have to get up. Checking my phone on the way down the stairs, Fe had been blowing up my phone. Swinging open the front door, it was Sameria, Cina's friend.

"Who the fuck just pops up at anybody's house this time of morning? What the fuck do you want? Cina ain't here!" I spat, losing my patience and cold as fuck from the cold ass air that just hit me in the face.

"I can't get in my house. I need to come in until the morning," Sameria said, bouncing on her toes, trying to stay warm as the snow blew in her face.

"Bitch, it's already the morning. You ain't coming up in here. You Cina's friend and like I told you, she ain't here. Take yo' ass up to the hospital until yo' momma let you in," I said, slamming the door in her face.

I made my way back upstairs. My phone started ringing and it was Pumpkin. I answered just in case something was going on with my lil brother. I would be up at the hospital, but I can't leave the house until 8 am. I called Susan's bitch ass to try to see if I could leave because my brother got shot and to tell her that I had contact with twelve. That bitch said she didn't care what was going on. If the house wasn't on fire, I couldn't leave.

"Wassup, Pump—"

"Nigga, don't wassup me. Let that girl in the fucking house. Are you crazy? Nigga, it's nine degrees outside! Let her in now!" Pumpkin screamed.

I made my way back downstairs, listening to Pumpkin scream about some shit that don't matter. "What's going on with my brother? Let me talk to him," I said as I swung open the front door and saw Sameria sitting on the porch curled up in a chair, crying while rocking back and forth. "Did you let that girl in the damn house, you fuckin' asshole?" Pumpkin screamed. After I told Pumpkin Sameria was in the house, she hung up on me.

"You better get yo' ass in this house before I shut this damn door and lock this bitch. It's too cold to be playing these types of fuckin' games with yo' ass!" I spat.

"Fuck you, R'Shad! This ain't yo' shit! This Pumpkin's house," Sameria said as she ran in the house, brushing past me.

"I see you brought yo' ass in here. Why you ain't with that lame ass nigga, Rodney?"

"The same reason why you ain't with that ratchet ass

bitch, Felicia. They both preoccupied with somebody else," Sameria said as a smirk spread across her face.

"Just because that nigga fucking bitches, making you cry and allowing them to disrespect you, don't speak on some shit you know nothing about. You can say some shit about Fe, but her fucking with another nigga is something that I ain't pressed about because that's me. What's mine, these niggas already know is off limits!" I spat, leaving her in the living room looking stupid.

"Fuck you and that bitch, but give me a fucking cover, so I can get some sleep. I'm fucking tired," Sameria said as she took off her coat and put her hair in a ponytail.

"Bitch, this ain't the motel that nigga Ro be taking you to. Freeze, hoe!"

"Felicia's the hoe!"

I went into the kitchen to get something to drink out of the icebox. I made my way back upstairs, so I could go to sleep. "Quit playing and get me a fucking blanket. It's freezing down here!" Sameria screamed up the stairs. I had to laugh. She had me fucked up thinking I was playing. The only reason I let her in the house is because of what's going on with Ricardo and that's what Pumpkin needs to be worried about. Otherwise, I would have left her ass on the porch and let her get fucking frostbite.

"I ain't playing. Use the cushions on the couch for a cover! You better take yo' ass to sleep! Be grateful you ain't outside in the blizzard. That's what's wrong with bitches now! Ungrateful as fuck!" I yelled back and got comfortable, so I could take my ass to sleep for a few more hours.

∾

"R'Shad, wake up." I heard somebody say as I stirred in my sleep. "R'Shad, wake up. The police are at the door," Sameria said as she went to touch me, trying to wake me up.

"Girl, don't fucking touch me. I don't know where the fuck yo' hands been," I said, snatching away the covers, so I could get up. "I thought you were supposedly so damn smart? How the fuck am I supposed to get up if yo' ass don't move?" I spat and brushed past her ass to go see what the fuck the police wanted.

"Fuck you, nigga! I am smart!" Sameria yelled.

I'm sure she is just nervous about fucking twelve being here. Not to say that I ain't, but after being locked up, it feels normal to always be around twelve. I made my way downstairs and two police officers were at the door. Opening the door, I could tell by the way they were looking at me that my ass was about to go to jail.

"Are you R'Shad Matthews?" One of the officers asked.

"Yea," I spat, knowing that I hadn't done shit for them to be looking for me.

"We have a warrant for your arrest," the officer said as he grabbed my left wrist, pushed me into the wall, and cuffed me while reading me my rights.

"What the fuck is you staring at me for? This ain't First 48 live, muthafucka, call Pumpkin!" I yelled at Sameria. She ran off as the police officer ushered me to the cop car.

We made it downtown fast and I was happy it was before three, so I could see a fucking judge and hopefully get the fuck out. I ain't did shit. If they were going to arrest me, why the fuck didn't they just do it last night? As

I sat waiting for the judge to call my name, it felt like time was going in slow motion. If it's not one thing, it's another. The fucked-up thing is I didn't even do shit to end up locked up again. My lil brother gets shot and I get locked up like I'm the one responsible for pulling the trigger.

"Calling case 18JD303, R'Shad Matthews," Gomez called as I was ushered by twelve to have a seat next to my client manager and across from the prosecutor.

"Why am I here?" I whispered to Susan.

"I'm asking for you to be remanded and to go back into custody."

"Are you fucking serious?" I asked, already knowing the answer.

"Your honor, R'Shad wasn't even out for a full twenty-four hours and he has already had contact with other felons as well as police contact, which are both violations of his parole that he didn't attempt to report," Susan said, looking straight ahead, refusing to look at me as I stared a hole through this wrinkly old bitch.

"R'Shad, what do you have to say for yourself?" Gomez asked.

"I had police contact because my house was shot up last night. I was celebrating coming home after being separated from my family for three years. I called Susan and talked to her, she's lying. As far as being around felons, none of my family are felons," I said.

At this point, I just accepted the fact that no matter what the fuck I say, I'm going back to jail. The only difference is this time, I'll be going to county jail instead of youth corrections because now I'm an adult. When I got offered a deal for that shit that happened with Reggie,

instead of just being released considering the circumstances, I lost faith in the system. Being locked up, the
way that I was treated and the fact that nobody seemed to
care or do anything to make changes, I already know that
this time won't be any different.

"Your honor, if you look at my revocation that I filed
with the court, you will see the statement from the
witness that the Denver Police department interviewed.
That is how we were made aware of everyone that was in
attendance at R'Shad's welcome home party," Susan said,
but this time she looked back at me.

"This is some bullshit!" Pumpkin yelled from
behind me.

"Ma'am, I'm going to ask you to be quiet or I'm going
to have you escorted out," Gomez said, like that wasn't
Pumpkin's first outburst.

"Your honor, what this comes down to is that R'Shad
does not have a safe environment to parole to. And with
him not being able to follow the rules for a full day, I am
requesting that he just complete six months, comes in
front of the court again and then we can make a decision
based off of his behavior and compliance to determine if
he should be released back into the community.

"Do you have anything that you would like to say, Mr.
Matthews, before I let you know my decision?" Gomez
asked as I sat up straight in my chair.

"It doesn't matter what the fuck I say because I'm
going back to jail for some shit that I had nothing to do
with. If I would have gotten shot instead, then y'all would
have just waited for me to heal and then locked me back
the fuck up. Just give me my time, so I can get it done,
shit," I spat.

I glanced back at Pumpkin and Fe as tears started to fall down both their faces. I know that Pumpkin has shed so many tears when it comes to me and my brother over the past few years. Not to mention, her son, my drunk ass cousin, who got picked up last night after he left the house drunk during the party. The judge said what I knew she was going to say, and Susan tried to talk to me about the next steps.

"Bitch, fuck you!" I spat as the police ushered me to the back.

9

CINA

Six Months Later...

"Cina, sit down and relax," Chaos said as I made sure that all the food was right for dinner.

"Shut up! If I didn't make sure that everything was right, you'd be talking shit with Pumpkin," I said, already knowing how this family is.

"I got it, you've done enough, and you need to sit down. Look at yo' feet. They all swollen, go sit down," Chaos said, now demanding.

Chaos isn't the type of nigga that will argue with me, so to stop myself from getting mad because he is always being too overprotective of me, I made my way out of the kitchen. Chaos wants everything to be perfect because Scar is coming home today. It's been six long months, but today is the day he's coming home. Scar didn't want a party because he said that shit was bad luck. None of us want a redo of what happened last time for sure, so it's just going to be us. We move into our new place next week and I'm so excited. Now we can get everything in place for our daughter. We finally found a place that we both liked, so it will do for now.

I've been staying at Pumpkins because I never went back to my mom's. I changed my number and I haven't talked to my mom since the night Chaos got shot. It hasn't been easy getting to where we are now. Chaos was in the hospital for two months, and he was in physical therapy for two months after that. I was scared that he was going to take longer to heal or never heal properly. When I told him I was pregnant once he was back home at Pumpkin's, he hit the streets hard. I've never seen somebody come up like he did and where Antonio slacked, he picked it up like it wasn't shit. He went from touching a lil money to being able to come up so good that he has his two traps that him and Antonio are running with the rest of their crew.

Antonio stays on bullshit and that just makes Chaos have to be gone more, which I hate. I'm used to being able to be with him all the time. He doesn't want me with him while he's handling business now and I don't like that shit.. One thing I can say is he always makes sure to make time for me and he manages to come home every night and still make it to school half the time.

"I don't give a fuck where you move, but you better have yo' ass in school, Chaos!" Pumpkin screamed.

"Pumpkin, I heard you the first time you said it!" Chaos yelled from the kitchen.

Chaos had a crackhead sign for our townhouse because Pumpkin wouldn't. She keeps saying that she doesn't care about Chaos leaving, but she doesn't want us to leave. Antonio is hardly ever here and when he is, he sleeps and is right back out. She'll have Scar here with her, so she won't be alone. Even though she is always talking shit about us being here I know that she likes for somebody to be here with here with her.

I texted Meria to make sure she was still coming over. She's leaving for school soon and she needs to be over here. Shit, she can bring Tasia with her. I already miss her and she ain't even left yet. I don't know how I'm going to deal with her being away. I'm happy for her because I know that she wants to get away from here. I'm just scared that once she leaves, we won't be as close as we are now.

"Sin said to come here. He around the corner at the park," Antonio said as he came in the house.

I slipped on my Nike slides and jumped up, so I could go and see him. Before my hand could touch the front door, Chaos was on my ass.

"Where are you going?" Chaos asked.

Turning around, I saw him unhooking his money phone from the charger.

"To see Sincere. Hurry up, Ricardo. I don't have all day," I said, walking out the house because I already know where this is headed.

I made my way around the corner jogging because he is taking this shit overboard, and I'm not waiting for anybody to tell me when I can move. Ever since Pumpkin's house got shot up and Chaos found out that I was pregnant, he wants to know where I'm at all times. If he can't be with me, he wants somebody he trusts with me. Since he's been at the house all day today, he's really on me. Nothing is going to happen to me, and he is really starting to get on my nerves with this shit.

"Cina, don't start this shit!" Chaos yelled as he pulled up aside me in his black Audi A8.

Rolling my eyes, I made my way over to the G-whip before he caused a fucking scene. When I got in, he didn't say shit and neither did I because we've had the same conversation so many times. Chaos and all his people are convinced that Rodney shot up the house, but he has been missing since the night that it happened. He hasn't been to school or any of his regular spots. I think that it was him now too because my cousin Lil Miller was all about the money and still is, so killing him wouldn't have gotten him anywhere.

Before Chaos could stop good at the park, I jumped out the car and jogged over to Sincere. It's like I just woke up one day and my stomach was big as hell. Trying to catch my breath, I sat down next to Sin at the picnic table. This was definitely something that I had to get used to, but I'm over it. I'm just ready to get my body back. I've never been this big and it has made me insecure as hell.

"I was about to leave before Rita be looking for me," Sin said as I hugged him.

I try to come and meet him over here at least every other day but with Chaos's new schedule, it doesn't always happen. Sin and I talked about what had been going on in the house, which is nothing new; my momma still on her same shit. As Sin and I talked, I looked over to see Chaos leaning against the car on the phone. Sin knows that I'm pregnant, but he hasn't told my momma because I told him that she can't know. She doesn't even know that we've been meeting each other.

Sin and I sat and talked for about thirty minutes and then he had to go. This part was always the hardest for me. I love my little brother and not being able to see him when I want bothers me. Not being able to be there to see for myself that he's good and being well taken care of makes me feel a way too. I slipped a knot of money into Sin's pocket as we hugged.

"Call me and let me know when you make it home," I said as Sin turned to walk away.

"Cina, chill out. I'm almost grown out here," Sin mentioned as he bounced his basketball.

I kept watching Sin walk until I couldn't see him anymore. I wish that Sin could just come and live with us, but I know that Rita will never let him. Tears started to well up in my eyes as Chaos ran over to me. I know that me leaving Rita's was what was best for me. There was no way I could have continued to live with her, and she was trying to convince me to set up my boyfriend.

"Cina, it's going to be okay. We'll be in our own place, soon. Sin can come through whenever, I already told you that. Stop crying man. I got us, I'm going to always make sure that my family is good, and Sin is fam, I got him too. I'll never lie to you, and I'll never be the reason why you cry. With everything that we've been through, if I told you I was going to do something, I made it happen," Chaos pleaded with me as he held me, and I continued to cry into his chest.

I've always been emotional, but I swear this pregnancy is making it so much worse. I been feeling like I cry about everything. This morning I was crying because Chaos forgot to bring me pumpkin seeds. Chaos has been dealing with my shit and I know it hasn't been easy, but he has been putting up with it. He's not the type of nigga to get an attitude and argue with me. He'll tell me what it is and listen to me, but even when I be trying to start an argument he'll shut me right the fuck down and will just start ignoring me

10

SAMERIA

"What the fuck are you doing here?" Scar spat as he walked into Pumpkin's.

"Nigga, I'm not here to see you," I said as Scar walked by and attempted to mush me.

He is the rudest nigga I've ever met. Felica came into the house looking me up and down, but she didn't say anything. Her facial expression said enough. The bitch is bothered that I'm over here, but I just came to spend more time with Cee. I'm going to miss her when I leave, but to be honest, I can't wait to get the fuck away from here. When I went and spent the weekend touring the college and getting familiar with the area, I loved it and everything about it. To be out of Colorado, I'm all for it.

I loved the fact that it was so many black people and everyone that I came in contact with was so friendly and showed so much love. And these were complete strangers. That southern hospitality shit is real. Growing up here in a predominately white state, it was something that I'm not used to but loved it. It was so refreshing to be away from home. Ever since I got back here, I been depressed because I just want to leave and never come back. Going to college was something that I always knew that I wanted to do. As things got worse at home with my momma, I knew that it was something I had to do in order to get a way and not end up miserable like her.

Tasia is with my grandma which is a relief because if she wasn't, she would be right here with me. I didn't really get to enjoy being a teenager because when other girls were going to school dances and going on dates, I was at home with Tasia. I was with Rodney for eight months and he didn't trip that I couldn't always be with him or that when I was able to sneak and meet up with him at the mall, Tasia was with me. But other niggas weren't even willing to give me a chance. Ever since that night Chaos got shot, I haven't talked to Rodney. He called and texted me, but I never replied. It took a lot for me to be done with him, but when I said I was done, I meant it and stuck to it.

"Bitch, where you been?" I asked as Cina and Chaos came in the door.

"My bad, Meria. Come upstairs, so I can show you the stuff that I got for the baby," Cina said as R'Shad made his way into the living room.

"Why is she always over here?" Felicia asked, looking me up and down but not talking to me.

"If you want to pay a bill in here, you can question who comes and goes in this muthafucka. If not, I suggest you just shut the fuck and be happy I let yo' ass up in here," Pumpkin spat, causing everybody to laugh but Felicia and R'Shad.

"Scar, are you going to let Pumpkin talk to me like that?" Fe whined.

"Man, chill out. Why the fuck would you even say some shit like that? You already know what it is. Don't start with this shit or yo' ass can go!" Scar spat.

"I already know from that one night that you like that bitch. Y'all must got something going on because the bitch is always over here," I heard Felicia say as we walked up the stairs.

"Bitch, did you hear that?" Cina asked me.

I rolled my eyes. I'm not thinking about R'Shad or Felicia's insecure ass. I don't give a fuck about R'Shad, and I know that he feels the same. Cina started showing me all the clothes they got for the baby. Turning around to leave the room so Cina can show me the clothes and toys in the other room, R'Shad was standing in the doorway, blocking me from leaving the room.

"Move, R'Shad, you can clearly see I'm trying to get out," I spat as attempted to push past him.

"You better learn some fuckin' manners. I don't know who the fuck you thought you were talkin' to, but I ain't that nigga," R'Shad replied still not budging.

"You need to learn some muthafuckin' manners because what I ain't —" I attempted to say before Chaos cut me off.

"Man, bra, chill. Let Meria out the damn room," Chaos said, moving R'Shad's arm.

I brushed past R'Shad, intentionally bumping him and made my way into the other room with Cina. I'm sick of his ass. Clearly, he should have stayed in jail a little longer and learned how to talk to people. He thinks that he can just say whatever the fuck he wants and it's okay.

He got the right one because I ain't scared of his ass, and we can definitely catch the heads.

As Chaos and R'Shad went into the room closing the bedroom door behind them, Cina finished showing me all the baby's stuff then we made our way downstairs to eat. Cina and I talked, and she told me about her ideas for their new place and how she wanted everything set up, showing me pictures of the stuff that they are going to have delivered to the new place. The only thing that is going to be hard for me is being away from Tasia, Cina and the baby. Cina and I talk and usually see each other every day. Not being able to do that is not going to be easy.

"Sameria!" Pumpkin screamed.

I made my way through the house to find her, checking my phone. Tasia and my grandma should be coming soon, but they hadn't called telling me they were on their way yet. Once I got to the porch, I saw the reason Pumpkin was calling my name. I don't know what was making me sicker, Pumpkin's cigarette or the fact that Zion was standing in front of me.

"How did you know where I was at?" I asked while twiddling with my fingers.

"Yo' momma told me you were probably over here," Zion said, flashing his perfect smile, showing his deep dimples.

"This ain't the damn love connection. And the last nigga you brought over here started some bullshit, so get the fuck off my porch!" Pumpkin said, swatting us away.

I led the way and Zion followed me outside to the front steps. I've been talking to Zion for about two months. He's really cool and I like him, but I'm leaving for college soon. He knows and even though he has expressed to me his feelings about not wanting me to leave, I am. I'll miss him and the times we shared, but I'm not getting caught up in my feelings about another nigga just for him to turn around and be just like the rest of them.

Zion is fine with his smooth caramel skin, light bright brown eyes, and thick full juicy lips that I love to kiss. He stood about 6'1 so he hovers over me. It's something about him that I just can't seem to get enough of. Zion is 19 and fine. He's that nigga that every bitch is turning their head to look at when he walks by. It's more than that to me because he was my friend before anything, and he supports me and all of my dreams.

"You fuck with her big head ass, Z?" R'Shad asked from behind me as he came down the stairs.

"Fuck you, R'Shad! Mind yo' fuckin' business!" I yelled. I rolled my eyes at R'Shad's comment as him and Zion shook up with each other.

I grabbed Zion by his arm and we walked down the street. Zion is cool, and I enjoy his company, but there is one thing that I could do without. His baby momma. After my last situation, a relationship is the last thing that I'm looking for, and I wish that he would just understand that.

"How do you know R'Shad?" I asked.

"We were locked up together. Did you think about what I said?" Zion said as he checked his phone.

"Yea, I did. It's not going to work. I'm leaving here and who knows when I'll be back. I'm not trying to put you in that type of situation," I said. Zion grabbed me and wrapped his arms around me as we continued to walk down the street.

"Fat- Fat, I ain't trying to hear that. I already told you what it was. I been trying to get at you for a minute. I already told you what it was. You going to school. Cool, I respect that. And I know that you are moving away ain't why you tryna just push a nigga to the side like this ain't more than what it is. It's something else that's holding you back and making you not want to fuck with a nigga. What is it?" Zion asked as we turned the corner.

"Really, nigga? This what you out here doing?" Nessa yelled as we walked past her and her dusty ass crew.

Rolling my eyes, I snatched away from Zion. He stopped to cut into Nessa as her friends started putting in their opinion. Zion ain't no hoe, and his mouth is slick. If he needs to go there with anybody he will without hesitation. Nessa is a big problem and Zion acts like it isn't, but it is. She is a bitch that just won't let go and the lengths that she will go in an attempt to get his attention are excessive and irritating as hell.

The bitch comments on everything that the nigga posts on social media and always has something to say about every move he makes. He says that it's nothing and to just ignore her, but it's only so much I can ignore. The thing is, he can't just stop all communication with Nessa because they have a daughter and I understand that. But her and her bullshit, I can't deal with.

"Fat- Fat!" Zion called out. I didn't even respond. I just kept on walking back around the corner to Pumpkin's.

We've known each other since we were kids; we grew up together. That is why his ass stay calling me Fat-Fat even though he knows I hate it. I was chubby when I was younger. Zion has been trying to get with me for a minute now and even when I was with Rodney, he didn't let up and was still shooting his shot. I never really paid him any attention and always kept him at a distance. I thought about giving him a chance awhile back because he was so persistent, but now lately, I've been thinking that it wasn't a good idea on my part even though it's only a temporary thing. I know that I can't deal with Nessa and her bullshit.

"Fat-Fat, why would you walk away?" Zion asked as he caught up with me, causing me to stop.

"You already know how I feel about Nessa and I'm not about to stand there why y'all go back and forth. Maybe y'all should just be together and be a family, shit," I said and started back walking.

"Look, I'm going to be there for my daughter, but you already know that I don't fuck with Nessa like that. I have to talk to her because she has my daughter, but I can't control the shit that she does or says. I don't want Nessa, and she already knows that. I want you, but you need to figure out what the fuck you want. You want me to put Nessa in her place, right? You keep talking that shit, but you don't even want to fuck with a nigga like that. You want me to do all this shit but I ain't good enough for you to even be my girl," Zion said as he walked away, leaving me standing in front of Pumpkin's.

I watched him walk over to R'Shad. I can't believe he's trying to flip this shit on me. I'll be happy when I get the fuck out of Colorado. I don't plan on ever coming back here. To be able to live my life and not have to worry about any of the bullshit that I've been dealing with is going to be everything.

"Bitch, what's wrong? What the fuck did Zion do?"

Cina asked as she wobbled down the steps to where I was standing.

"The same shit that I was telling you about. Look, here come that bitch now," I said, pointing as Nessa walked around the corner pushing their daughter in her stroller.

11

CHAOS

"Ricardo, be careful," Pumpkin said as I slipped on my shoes to go outside.

"Pumpkin, I'm not going nowhere but outside," I said, shaking my head.

Every time I leave the house, P be trippin' and worrying. It's always some bullshit that seems to go down, so I know why Pumpkin be trippin'. She actin' like she can't wait for us to get out, but she been talking so much shit with it getting closer to time for us to leave. I'm happy as fuck that my brother is home. She'll have somebody else to stalk because I love P, but she be doing too much sometimes.

"Cee, some girl just called and said some shit about she's going to be late," I said. I kissed Cina on the cheek and made my way across the street.

"I'm so sick of bitches playing with my time," Cina whined from behind me.

I turned around and looked at her. We've had this conversation several times. I keep telling her to stop fucking with half these bitches because of how they try to play her. She knows I don't want to hear about the shit because I've already had to cut into several bitches about playing with her time. Then I'll come home a week later, and she'll be doing the same bitches' nails. I just get sick of hearing her complain about that shit, so when I get sick of the shit, bitches get cussed the fuck out. If I do business with their niggas, they get cut the fuck off and can't get money with me. I know that this is what she wants to do and she's cold, so I support her all the way.

"Cee, Yoni called!" I yelled across the street as Scar introduced me to Zion.

"This my little brother, Ricardo," Scar said as I looked at him up and down.

"Wassup," I said to Zion as I sparked my blunt.

"Nigga, you are my little brother. What the fuck, you think you the big brother nigga?" Scar said, laughing as I tried to pass him the blunt.

"You Chaos, right?" Zion asked as I hit the blunt again, letting the smoke fill my lungs since Scar didn't want to hit it.

"Yea," I said as I glanced across the street at Sameria sitting on the steps mugging in our direction.

Cina and I talk about everything, so I know that Sameria fucks with this nigga Zion, but this is my first time ever talking to him. I'm not hitting no blunt after no nigga that I don't know, so I didn't offer Zion to hit my shit. He keeps looking at my shit but looking is all his ass will be doing. Scar and Zion finished chopping it up, and Zion made his way across the street with Sameria.

"Damn, so what the fuck done happened in the few

months that I been gone?" Scar asked, looking at my watch.

"Shit, a lot, bra. With Cina being pregnant, I had to make some shit happen. Play time is over and I have to make sure they are good no matter what," I said, meaning every word.

Scar shook his head, taking it all in. Scar and I talked to each other all the time, but we never discussed what I was doing out here. He would say shit here and there, letting me know that he heard 'bout what I was doing. I wasn't surprised, muthafuckas love to talk. Especially about shit that don't concern them and they don't even know the truth about. Scar and I sat and chopped it up about everything that had been going on lately.

"Scar, I need you to do this shit with me," I said after going over the shit in my head for the hundredth time.

"Bra, I don't know," Scar said as he ran his hands over his face.

"Look, I'm telling you, the money that I'm getting is a'ight, but it can get better. With us doing this shit, we can really get some money. I know you ain't trying to stay with Pumpkin for too long."

"I don't know, bra, I got to think about it. I mean, shit. I ain't gon' lie, I been thinking about that shit, but I have to think some more on it. On some real shit, what the fuck is up with this nigga doe?" Scar said, pointing across the street and then putting his hands back in his pockets.

Looking across the street, Antonio's drunk ass was arguing with a bitch in front of the house. It's always some shit with this nigga. He's family so I been letting shit slide, but this shit is getting out of control. This nigga got too many damn problems with his bitches that keep ending up here where the fuck we lay our head at.

"Muthafucka, take that shit down the street. You and that dusty ass bitch!" Scar spat.

"Nigga, you shut the fuck up! You don't know who you fucking talking to! I will call some niggas over here to beat—" Tay screamed, but shut the fuck up mid-sentence as I had to pull Scar back from going across the street.

"Bitch, the only thing saving you is Pumpkin being right there! What type of nigga would bring this shit in front of his momma house? Nigga, you a fucking clown!" Scar yelled, snatching away from me and making his way across the street.

"Bra, chill," I said as I jogged across the street, throwing my blunt because I know with my brother how the fuck this could go.

"Ricardo, don't fucking touch me!" Scar spat before I could even get close to him.

"You gotta go! You nor that hoe can come in here," Pumpkin said as she walked over to where Antonio and Tay were leaning against a car.

"Ma, for real? You gon' kick me out?" Antonio screamed.

"Lower yo' fucking voice when talking to her!" Scar spat.

"Antonio, chill the fuck out," I said, losing my patience.

"Yes, go get yo'self together and then you can come home. That bitch not coming back up in my house," Pumpkin said.

"This is my fuckin' girl! You know what, fuck it! And

fuck you, Ma, be—" Antonio attempted to say before Scar hit him, causing him to fall to the ground hard.

Scar hit him a few times. He pulled him by the collar of his white t-shirt, held him with one hand and was fucking him up with the other, rotating hands. After a few minutes, Scar felt that he had enough and dropped him to the ground then made his way in the house. Pumpkin followed behind him while asking him was he okay. Tay waited until Scar was in the house before she even moved to check on Antonio. I turned to make my way in the house.

"Chaos!" Antonio called after me, slurring his words. I turned around and just looked at Antonio. Me and him have been arguing about the shit that he does with bitches, the way he talks to Pumpkin and how he has been handling business. We didn't have these issues when we were just getting a few dollars but ever since this nigga been getting a bag, he can't handle it, and it's making me question fucking with him.

"I don't got shit to say to you. You need to get yo'self together. It doesn't make no sense for you to come around here or show yo' face at none of the spots until you get yo' shit right," I said, meaning every word. I looked at Antonio in disgust at how this nigga done turned into a fucking disaster in just a few months.

"Cuz, we family, you can't do me like this. What the fuck am I supposed to do? How the fuck am I supposed to feed my girl? I got a fucking baby on the way. You can't do me like this," Antonio pleaded.

"Give me the fucking keys," I said, walking up on Antonio.

He had one hand wrapped around Tay. He was all

fucked up. He had blood leaking from his mouth, covering his white teeth. His yellow face was red like a fucking stop sign and parts have turned blue and purple from Scar fucking him up. His left eye was so swollen, he couldn't even open it. I don't even want to look at him like this, but he already knew what was coming when he kept talking crazy to Pumpkin.

"You can't do this to me. Man, Chaos, hear me out," Antonio pleaded as I ran his pockets.

Once I found the phone that we used for business and his keys, I checked his key ring to see that the trap house keys and the keys to Pumpkin's were all that's on the ring. Antonio kept trying to get me to hear him out, but I didn't even waste my time responding. When he gets his shit together, he can come back, and we can continue getting money. Until then, it ain't shit that we can discuss.

"What did Yoni want?" I asked Cina as I walked in the house.

Cina and Sameria were sitting in the living room watching tv, but even with the tv blasting, they could barely hear the shit with how loud Pumpkin was scream- ing. Scar didn't want to have a party because he didn't want any shit but sure enough, on his first day out, we got a bunch of bullshit going on. It's always something goin' on over here. Cina doesn't complain about the shit with Antonio to me, but I know that she be talking shit to Sameria. Cina was smiling, but still hadn't answered my question as I stood there waiting for an answer.

"I'm not telling you," Cina said.

I laughed because I already knew what my cousin Yoni wanted, but Cina was acting like it was a secret. Yoni is going to let Cina work in her shop and get her license under her to be a nail tech. That way she could work under her and get all her hours needed to be able to take the test to be licensed when she's ready. It was Yoni's idea, but I know that is exactly what Cina needs. I made my way to the kitchen to check on Pumpkin because I knew she was mad as hell.

"Don't fucking tell me how to raise my son! When was the last time you were around? When was the last time you even seen him? He only calls you when we get into! Did he tell you what the fuck he has been doing?" Pumpkin screamed into the phone.

By what Pumpkin was saying, I knew she was talking to Big Tone, Antonio's dad. Him and Aunt Pumpkin were together when I first moved in here, but after a few months, they went their separate ways. I remember hearing him telling her to just let me go to the state, she didn't need to be worrying about me or Scar, and that she had her own son to worry about. During that time, I remember just saying fuck it and packed up my shit to run away.

When Pumpkin came into my room and saw that I had packed up all my shit, she put Big Tone out her house that same night. He used to come and get Antonio on the weekends and shit, but that stopped. I haven't seen him in years. On some real shit, I didn't even know that Antonio still talked to him. Especially the way that he talked bad about him all the time.

"Muthafucka, when I put you out my house, I was done listening to yo' muthafuckin' opinion. If you want to give Antonio some advice, then you do that. What the fuck goes on in my house is my business and I don't give a fuck what you or anybody have to say! Bitch, pay that back-child support than give me call!" Pumpkin screamed, threw her phone on the kitchen table and stormed out.

I hate screaming and arguing, always have. Scar just sat there eating like nothing was even going on around him. Even with all the shit that just happened, this nigga ain't fazed by none of it. I sat down at the table with him and checked the phone that I got from Antonio.

"That shit still bothers you, don't it?" Scar asked, catching me off guard.

"What are you talking about?" I asked, not looking up from the phone.

"When people are yelling and fighting?" Scar asked, and I could feel him staring at me.

"Naw, I'm good, but I don't like that shit. I can't deal with the yelling and shit," I said, looking up at him.

"Then how the fuck you been livin' with Pumpkin for so long? All she does is scream. She doesn't know how to talk in a normal tone," Scar said and we both laughed.

"Don't be in here talking shit about me. That girl is at the door and if she come in starting shit, I'm going to drag her out the house by that cheap ass ponytail," Pumpkin said, peeking her head in the doorway of the kitchen.

"Could you let her in?" Scar asked.

"I'm not, the bitch ain't here to see me. Plus, the bitch can't come in here until she gives Cina her money for doing her nails. Right, Ricardo?" Pumpkin said, looking at me.

I got up and made my way through the living room and upstairs. Cina and Sameria were still sitting there talking and watching TV. She not my bitch and if she didn't have the money, Cina shouldn't have done her nails. Cina always trying to look out and help mutha-fuckas. That is one of the reasons that I love her, but her and these bitches gon' learn today. I made my way upstairs, found what I was looking for and made my way downstairs. Cina asked me where I was going as I walked out the front door and closed it behind me. I didn't answer her. I could hear her talking shit, but I didn't waste my time responding.

When I walked outside, Felicia was sitting on the front steps. It was hot as hell outside, so hot that sweat dripped down her face as the sun beamed on us.

"Where the fuck is R'Shad?" Felicia asked.

I reached in my pocket and grabbed out the tool that I've seen Cina use to cut down nails. I grabbed Felicia's left hand and started cutting them bitches off.

"What the fuck are you doing? Get off of me!" Felicia screamed and tried to squirm out of my grip. I gripped her hand tighter with my left hand and proceeded to cutting the rest of her nails off. The harder I squeezed on her wrist, Felicia got quiet and stopped telling me to stop.

"Ricardo, for reals? What the fuck are you doing? It's not that serious," Cina said as I walked back up on the porch where she was standing watching me.

"It is that serious. If the bitch ain't got no money, then she don't get shit," I said then made my way in the house and handed her the tool.

"Huh, yo' bitch gone need a few," I said, tossing a pack of Band-Aids at Scar and made my way upstairs to get in the shower, so I could go check on my traps.

12

SCAR

"You just got out and you about to be out with Chaos all fucking night? What about me?" Felicia whined.

"We done already had this conversation. You already know what the fuck it is," I said. I snatched my phone off the dresser and made my way out of the room with Fe on my heels.

"That has nothing to do with the fact that I don't want you to leave," Felicia whined, brushing past me and running to the front door of her apartment.

I'd only been out three days and shit been fucked up since my first day out. Felicia is my bitch and nothing or nobody could ever come in between the bond that we have. She has held a nigga down when I didn't really have nobody but my family. I love Felicia, but her thinking that I'm about to sit in this fucking house with her all day and night, she out her fucking mind. Looking at Felicia with her arms folded across her chest, she was mugging the fuck out of me.

Fe is bad as fuck. She has light skin, blonde hair and

some sexy, chinky eyes. Felicia is short, skinny and has just enough ass for me. Fe is more than just my girl, she's my best friend. Felicia was my girl before I caught my case. When I got sentenced, I didn't think that we would make it, but she proved me and everybody else wrong.

"Fe, move! I don't have time for this shit right now!" I spat, losing my patience.

"I'm not fucking moving. You not about to choose Chaos over me!"

"Her, we go with this shit. I'm not about to keep having the same fucking conversation with you. I'm not choosing my lil brother over you, this is about some money. Do you want me to be yo' bum, Felicia?" I asked and picked Fe up with her kicking and screaming as I moved her away from the door.

"I'm coming with you!" Felicia said, snatching up her purse.

"Felicia, sit the fuck down! Watch some TV, read a fucking book!" I spat and slammed the door behind me.

I jogged to the car that Chaos was sitting in. He'd been blowing up my phone. I'm surprised that he was even sitting out here still. I'd been thinking long and hard about what my lil bra and I had discussed. I went and looked for a job the day after I got out, but none of that shit wasn't going to get it. Pumpkin been on me and doesn't want me in the streets but shit, after seeing everything that Ricardo has on the floor, I told him that I would come and check shit out tonight.

"What the fuck took you so long?" Ricardo asked as I got in the car.

"Felicia on some bullshit."

"Pumpkin wants you to come home," Chaos said as he skirted off.

After the shit happened with me and Antonio getting into, I decided to just go and stay with Fe for a few days. She wants me to live with her, but right now that ain't going to work. I can't see myself being the type of nigga just living off my bitch. She just wants a nigga to stay in the house all day up under her. That ain't me and she already knows that.

"Felicia want you to be her bitch," Chaos said in between taking pulls from his blunt.

"Fuck you! I ain't gon' be nobody bitch. Everybody ain't with the shits like, Cina," I said as we pulled up into an apartment complex.

"You and Felicia both act like she ain't a fucking rat. I know you love her and all, but she just playing a role because you out now. She gon' be back on her shit real soon," Ricardo said as he opened his door.

I know that Felicia be boosting. That ain't no surprise to me. However, when Pumpkin and Ricardo be talking, it seems like they want to say some shit but be beating around the bush about it. That shit doesn't sit right with me. Ricardo... I can't say that I'm surprised that nigga be bottling shit up and then just end up flipping out when he's had enough. Pumpkin, on the other hand, she doesn't hold back shit, so I wonder why the fuck she ain't saying all that's on her mind.

"Where Cina at?" I asked, texting Fe back as I got out the car.

"She at the house with Pumpkin. She's used to being able to be with me all the time. I don't want her out here and she carryin' my daughter and shit."

"Speak yo' mind. What the fuck is yo' real issue with Felicia?" I said because I can't keep biting my tongue, it just ain't me.

Ricardo stopped walking and turned to face me. The look he gave me is a look that he has given me many times over the years. I remember having to make him say shit our entire life. He has never been a real talkative nigga, but me, I'm gon' say whatever the fuck is on my mind because I'm not letting a muthafucka slide with shit.

"I don't give a fuck about Felicia stealing, nigga, I steal. Felicia just ain't the bitch that you think she is."

"Nigga, stop playing with me and say what the fuck is on yo' mind!" I spat.

"Nigga, I heard her on the phone the other night telling somebody that sheabout to get it, so you don't fuck with me or Pumpkin and get you linked with her people. Is that what the fuck yo' plan is now?"

"Nigga, have I ever not had yo' back? You think that I'd choose anybody over y'all. For real, nigga?" I spat and Ricardo turned to walk away.

I followed behind Ricardo and spoke to a few muthafuckas as we walked through the apartment complex. Fe been coming at me about linking with her brother. I ain't never really rocked with her brother. It's something about that nigga that just ain't never sit right with me. He the type of nigga that just always been a trick with bitches, and niggas always taking shit from him. That ain't the type of nigga that I'm going to do business with, I don't give a fuck who he is. Felicia and I been bumping heads about it, but her telling anybody some slick shit like that ain't cool. I'll deal with her ass when I get back to the house.

It makes sense why I haven't heard from Pumpkin all day and when I called her, she didn't answer. We made it to the apartment and Ricardo pulled out his key. Walking in the trap, I could smell food cooking. The smell caused me to stop in my tracks because there is only one person that I know whose house always smells like this. Ricardo made his way through the house, and I posted up by the door. I'm real skeptical about being around new people. It takes me forever to trust new people, and I don't know who all in here, but I could hear somebody talking.

"Baby! Welcome home!" My God mom, Tricky, screamed as she came running in the living room.

"Wassup, God Mom," I said as she hugged me tight.

Tricky and my mom were tight as hell and she is me and Ricardo's god-mom. When I walked in the house, so many memories started running through my head, thinking about my momma and Tricky. Tricky sent me cards and wrote me letters, but I didn't know that this was one of my brother's spots. I didn't even know that he still talked to Tricky.

"Where is Felicia at? Let me go and make you a plate. Pumpkin told me that she couldn't cook, so that's why I cooked. I'm so happy that you're finally home. Yo' momma would be so happy," Tricky said as she made me a plate.

I sat in a barstool and picked up a picture of my momma sitting on the island that separates the living room from the kitchen. On Sunday, in two days, is the day that momma died. It's never an easy day for me, but I know that it's even harder for Ricardo, but he never speaks on it to me. Tricky and I talked and caught up. Tricky never had any kids, but she always kept several niggas on her team. From the shit that she got on, I know she is going to see one of them. With her old ass.

"Okay, I got to go, I have a date. I'll see you Sunday at Pumpkin's. Be careful both of y'all. I love y'all," Tricky said, sitting my plate in front of me and making her way out the door.

"Tricky, you too damn old to be still trickin'," I said in-between getting into this bomb ass macaroni.

"Nigga, I ain't too fucking old for nothing. Mind the muthafucking business that pays you, R'Shad. Bring Felicia with you next time you come by," Tricky said as the door closed behind her.

A few minutes after Tricky walked out the door, somebody started knocking at the door. Coming home and seeing what my brother is running is weird as hell. He's always been a laid-back nigga and never did too much talking. Seeing him running shit and giving orders is some shit I never thought I would see. He ain't the same lil nigga I left behind, and that shit is going to take some time getting used to.

"Nigga, get the door, this is fucking training! Pick up that fucking plate and take it to the door if you need too!" Ricardo screamed from the back.

"Now you want to speak up. Say it wit' yo' chest lil nigga!" I said as I jumped up to get the door.

Growing up the way that we did, we were introduced to a bunch of shit that we should have never seen. I'm not surprised that Ricardo chose to be in the game. Growing up, the niggas that were selling dope were the only niggas that had anything and wasn't struggling to get by where we lived. The shit that I didn't know about being a fucking criminal, I damn sure learned it while I was locked up.

"What you want?" I asked the crackhead as he kept counting the same three bills like they were going to change.

"Where is Chaos at?" He asked as he started rocking back and forth.

"Chaos!" I screamed and sat back down.

I don't have no patience and no matter how much I try to work on that shit, it doesn't seem to ever get better. I be done knocked this fucking crackhead out because he is irritating me taking too long to decide what he wants. The smell coming from him was fucking with my stomach and making me lose my fucking appetite.

"This my brother, Scar. This is, Sticks," Ricardo said and made his way out the room.

"What the fuck you want?" I asked as I hopped off the barstool.

"Let me get uh, uh, uh, uh—" Sticks attempted to say before I cut him off.

"A what nigga? I don't have all fucking night to be standing here waiting for you!" I spat.

"Let me just get uh, uh a twenty, but all I got is fifteen."

"You ain't got twenty, you ain't getting a twenty. Nigga, this ain't name yo' price."

"You look familiar. You look like somebody I know."

"Nigga, I don't care who the fuck I look like. All you need to worry about is what the fuck you want, so you can get the fuck on."

Knock, knock, knock!

"Sticks, what the fuck is you doing still here? Nigga, you be doin' too much fucking talking," Chaos said as he walked around us and answered the door.

"You look like my brother," Sticks said, pointing his finger.

I snatched two tens out of Stick's hand and went to get what he paid for. Ricardo told me about all of the hiding spots in both his traps, so I knew exactly where to go. Going down the hall and walking into the bedroom, I snatched up Sticks' shit then made my way back to the living room.

"Huh. Now get the fuck out," I said, handing Sticks his shit.

"You look just like my brother and you got a smart-ass mouth just like that muthafucka too," Sticks said on his way out the door.

"Take a fucking bath before you come back through here!" I spat and looked at my phone because it was lighting up on the counter.

"Scar, this is Unique. Unique, this is my brother," Ricardo said.

"Hey!" Unique said, too damn happy for me.

I didn't respond to Unique. I don't do too much talking to bitches. I finished eating and put my phone back down because I was not about to argue with Felicia all fucking night. I came to see if I wanted to rock with my brother and this is what the fuck I'm worried about right now. Ricardo was sitting down discussing some shit with Unique.

"Yo' rude ass could speak back," Unique said as she stood up to leave.

"Yea, bitch, I could have!" I spat.

"Who are you calling a bitch?" Unique screamed.

"Bitch, you. Go practice drawing on y'o fucking eyebrows and get the fuck out my face!" I spat as Ricardo started laughing.

Ricardo and I set in the trap all night until the sun came up. People were in and out; that shit made time start flying by. The money that we made was just as easy as Ricardo said it would be. I have to go and talk to Pumpkin because she still ignoring me. If it was anybody else, I wouldn't give a fuck, but because it's Pumpkin, I need to go and talk to her.

Ricardo locked up Tricky's, and we made our way out. I knew that Cina had made runs and shit for this nigga, but I didn't know her cousin Unique was too. I'm still playing this shit in my head while I decide if I'm going to do this shit or not. It's gon' to have to be some changes if I'm going to get in this shit with him. One of them is that bitch with them scary ass eye brows.

13

SAMERIA

"Where is Cina at?" My momma asked as she stood in the doorway of my room.

"She'll be over here in a little bit," I said as I checked my phone to see if Zion had texted me back.

"We need to talk," my momma said as she plopped down on my bed.

I didn't respond, I just kept curling my hair. My momma hadn't said anything, but I could see her mugging me from my vanity mirror. I turned around, so she could say whatever the fuck she had to say and then leave me the fuck alone. She took off work today and tomorrow which surprised the fuck out of me. My graduation party is tomorrow and her and my God mom, Joy, are getting everything together.

"I know that you think that I be trippin' and I be hard on you, but I'm not. Everything that I do is for you and Tasia. I bust my ass to make sure that both of y'all are good. You think that you're being punished because you couldn't be in the streets every day and night with Cina. Watch how that shit plays out with her and that lil boy. It's not going to end good," my momma said, waiting for an answer.

"I know that you have to work, and I appreciate everything that you do for us, ma. I'm not gon' lie, I do get sick of having to watch Tasia every day. If I do get to go and do something, I always have to take Tasia with me," I said, feeling relieved to say it to her finally.

"What I'm not going to do is apologize. Me going to work every day is ensuring that yo' ass is going to that college. I've made sure that you never have to be in a position to depend on a nigga for a muthafucking thing. See, that is where I fucked up. When yo' dad was killed, I didn't have shit, and I had to start all over because I had put myself in a fucked-up position.

"Ma, I'm not going to do that," I said and for once wishing that she was at work.

"That's what you say now, but all it takes is the right nigga with the right words that will have you caught up and in a fucked-up position that isn't going to be easy to get out of. Sameria, I love you, but I also know that the niggas you been choosing are the same type of niggas that you need to stay the fuck away from. Why not be with a nigga that ain't in the streets.? Why would you want to fuck with a nigga that when he leaves, you don't know if he's coming back?"

"Momma, I'm not even talking to Rodney anymore. We've been done."

"I'm not talking about Rodney's no-good ass. I'm talking about Zion, Sameria. That nigga is not the one and you deserve better than that."

"We're just friends," I said, not wanting to talk about him either.

"Don't end up pregnant by yo' friend, Sameria."

"Momma, I got a question."

"Get to it, girl. I have to go and finish making these cakes."

"Who killed my dad?" I sighed, hoping that today she will finally give me an answer.

"It doesn't matter. What's done is done," my mom said as she jumped up and left the room.

I'm not surprised. She will never talk about my dad and that's why I tried to ask today. Usually she won't even mention him, like he never even existed. My momma never got over my dad and her heart was never the same, even after all of this time. Even though she never talks about him, she still has all of his clothes hanging in the closet like he left it and all of his shoes are on the shoe rack in her room. She never removed any of his stuff and I think that looking at it every day just makes it worse, but I'll never tell her that.

"I can't believe yo' momma is here," Cina said as she plopped down on my bed.

"You are big as hell, Cee," I said and busted out laughing.

"Fuck you! You better be lucky that I love you because I wanted to stay in the bed. I didn't feel like moving. I was at the shop last night all night," Cina said as she laid back on my bed.

"Did y'all get everything together at the new place?" I asked as Joy walked into my room.

"My baby is leaving for school! What am I going to do without you?" My god mom whined loud as hell.

"You took forever to get here. Why you tell my momma about Zion?" I said as I jumped up to hug Joy.

"You need to talk to yo' momma and tell her about what you got going on. I ain't getting in the middle of y'all shit. Tasia told her about that nigga, not me. I don't be telling Susie's ass what you be telling me. I don't like him, and you already know that. You know who you should get with and Cina can hook you up," Joy said as a smile spread across her face.

"I'm not fucking with nobody here. I'm' bout to be leaving for school. I'm done with Denver niggas," I said, meaning every word.

"Fuck what you talkin' about. That young boy Scar is fine as hell."

"Aw hell naw, you trippin'. You don't know nothin' 'bout him. That nigga is rude as hell, and he crazy. Utt unn, I'm good on him," I said as I straightened up my vanity.

"Bitch, what you want, a punk? Somebody to paint yo' nails and hold yo' purse?" Joy said as Cina busted out laughing.

"I think y'all would be cute together and from what I heard, him and Felicia ain't working out," Cina threw in her two cents.

Me and my mom haven't been close in years, but my God mom and I have always been tight. Nothing will ever change that. I tell her everything and I know she be telling my momma shit, even though she says she doesn't. She got a new job recently, and I don't get to see her as much as I used to, but she always calls or texts to make sure that I'm good. I'm not trying to hear shit about Scar's rude ass. Felicia can have that.

Joy made her way downstairs. Cina and I caught up as Cina looked through the stuff that I bought yesterday. I'd been getting all my stuff together because I leave in a few weeks, and I want to have everything together when it's time for me to leave. My momma and Joy are driving me to Texas. I'm glad that Joy is going with us, otherwise it would be a long ass ride.

"What's wrong?" I asked. All of a sudden, Cina had gotten quiet.

"Bitch, what am I going to do when you leave? You gon' forget about me and go get some new friends. Then all Chaos wants me to do is sit in the house."

"Bitch, I'm not going to get no new friends. You still gon' be my bitch. Bitch, you got a lot going for yo'self, even though you not graduating yet. You been going to school like you're supposed to, so you'll be able to get all the credits that you need to get back on track. You'll be done in no time, Cee. Bitch, and you working in the shop with Yoni!" I said as I sat on the bed next to her.

"I know, and you know that I been wanting to get in a shop, but the thing is, I'm scared, Sameria. What if I'm not a good mom? What if I ain't good at being a mom like Rita? What if I can't do this, Meria and you not even going to be here with me?" Cee said, pouting, sitting up and laying her head on my shoulder.

"You got this and you're going to be a great mom. You ain't Rita, Cee. You're not going to be like her. Quit stressing out about Sincere too, he's going to be good. You a fucking cry baby, Cee. I'm so ready for you to have my niece, so you can get back to being Bonnie because, bitch, you are turning into a punk."

"Fuck you, I'm not no punk. Bitch, I'll fight you and

anybody else," Cina said serious as hell.

"Yea, bitch, in a few months. No time soon, hoe!" I said, laughing.

"Y'all hoes come down here! I didn't graduate high school, and I'm not doing everything for this damn party!" Joy yelled up the stairs.

I'm going to miss Cee and being able sit with her for hours and do everything with her. It's easy for me to say that things won't change in our friendship, but I don't really know because I won't be here. I'll come home for breaks, but a lot of stuff is about to change for both of us because she's going to be a mom soon. We made our way downstairs. Unique was down there and Joy had already put her to work. Even though a lot of the stuff is done, we still have a lot to do in order to be ready for tomorrow.

"Look, bitch!" Unique said, catching my attention as I took pictures with my family.

Looking around, my eyes landed on Zion and his daughter. It's weird to see all these people that I haven't seen in years. My mom invited all of my dad's family and hers. My mom refused to accept any help from her family because she didn't want them to throw it up in her face that they did anything for us. My grandma comes around here and there and will get Taisa sometimes, but that's it. So, I'm still trying to figure out why she invited any of them here.

"Those muthafuckas just came to be nosy. When is the last time you even seen these muthafuckas?" Joy spat in between us taking a picture.

"Why did she even invite them?" I asked.

"To show them that you made it and didn't need shit from them. Being petty," Joy said as my momma looked at both of us crazy.

"I thought you were done with him. Why is he here?" Joy asked, pointing across the backyard.

Looking over, I saw Rodney walking in with gifts in his hands. I hadn't seen Rodney or talked to him, so to see him here right now, I'm really confused. Why he would think it was okay for him to show up now? My momma met Rodney, but because of the type of nigga that he was, she never liked him. I was sneaking around still seeing him even though I knew how my momma felt, but because of her work schedule, it worked.

"Bitch, um, what the fuck is Rodney doing here?" Cina whispered in my ear.

"Bitch, you got bigger problems. Scar and Chaos supposed to be coming," Unique whispered.

This is the last thing I need and the way that Zion is mugging me, I know I'm going to have to hear his mouth too. I made my way over to where Rodney was standing, talking to my cousin Zeek. I grabbed Rodney's arm and led the way to the front of my house.

"Why the fuck are you here?" I spat loud enough for him to hear over the music.

"Damn, after all this time, that's how you feel? I thought you loved a nigga, but I see that all that shit went out the window. I see Zion is here. You need to just tell that nigga to get the fuck on. Daddy's home!"

"Daddy's home? Nigga, you got me all the way fucked up. My dad is dead and nigga, I been done with you, and you already know that. Wherever the fuck you been, I suggest you go back because I'm still not fucking with you."

"Damn, nigga, where you been?" Scar asked as him, Chaos and some other nigga that I don't know surrounded us.

"Nigga, I been around. You ain't been looking too hard. Nigga, I ain't hard to find!" Rodney spat with an attitude like he hadn't been hiding like a bitch.

"Sameria, go back to yo' party," Scar said, trying to shoo me away.

"Nigga, this is my house. You can't tell me where the fuck I can and can't be in my yard. Take yo' ass back up the street giving orders!" I replied+.

Chaos nor the other nigga said shit. Scar was doing all the talking, but the baseball bat Chaos was swinging spoke volumes. Scar thinks that he can say whatever the fuck he wants to anybody and they supposed to just jump and do whatever he says. He gets disrespectful and them muthafuckas do whatever he says without a problem. I'm not one of them muthafuckas that he can intimidate. I don't give a fuck how crazy he is and how many times he been to jail.

Scar stepped in-between Rodney and me and started looking in the bags that Rodney had. What the fuck is wrong with this nigga? Rodney's punk ass all of sudden had nothing to say. Scar could snatch all these bags and balloons from him right now, and I don't think his punk ass would do anything. What the fuck was I ever thinking fucking with this nigga?

"Where the fuck did you get this shit from, an outlet, nigga? You want some of this cheap shit?" Scar asked, looking back at me and knocking all the bags and balloons out of Rodney's hands.

"Naw, I want him and yo—" I attempted to say before Scar picked me up, throwing me over his shoulder.

"Put me down!" I spat with my ass in the air and him squeezing me tight as we made our way through the front door of my house.

"Shut the fuck up, or I'm not putting you down!" Scar spat.

"Put me the fuck down now," I said just loud enough for him to hear me because I don't want to hear my mommas' mouth or none of these long-lost relatives that are here.

"Tell me that you're sorry for not following my directions and for fucking with a broke ass nigga," Scar said, serious as hell.

"I guess you won't be putting me down because I'm not apologizing for shit. Nigga, you really are crazy," I said.

"Put that fucking girl down. Don't be over here embarrassing me," Pumpkin said from behind us.

Scar put me down real fast. I pulled down my dress and got myself together, so I could get back to my party.

"I can't stand you, R'Shad! Don't fuckin' ruin my fucking party!" I spat before Pumpkin and I made our way to the backyard.

"Fuck you! I asked you to go back to the party first before yo' lil boyfriend get beat the fuck up and kidnapped. Ungrateful bitches!" Scar spat like I was in the wrong for being upset.

As I made my way back to the backyard, Cina and Unique rushed over to me and Pumpkin. Pumpkin doesn't fuck with Unique at all, so she hurried up and made her way to speak to my mom and Joy. Looking around the party, I saw Zion feeding his daughter and talking to my cousin Zeek. I'm surprised that he even showed up the way that I cut into him, letting him know the last time that I saw him would be the last time. I hope one day I can meet a nigga that can put up with my attitude like Zion.

"Bitch, I seen R'Shad pick you up. What the fuck is going on with y'all?" Unique asked as Cina started laughing.

I left Cina and Unique standing there talking shit and made my way over to Zion. My mom went to call my name, but I saw Joy stopping her. When I sat down next to Zion, he didn't even acknowledge that I was sitting next to him. I guess I did deserve that because of how I came at him the last time we talked. To be honest, I just don't want to get caught up in my feelings more than I already have because I'm leaving.

"Nessa and I had a conversation, and she won't be an issue anymore. She knows what it is, and I made it be known that she is going to have to start respecting you. I was in the wrong for not doing that from day one, but with you constantly throwing it in a nigga's face that you leavin' and this is some temporary shit, that is why I handled shit the way I did," Zion said, breaking the silence between us.

Zeek got up and made his way back over to the food. I didn't say anything right away because I didn't want to come off being fucked up. I don't think that Zion and I can do anything long distance, and I don't want to get hurt again. Who knows when will be the next time we even see each other after I leave? It's easy to say that we'll make it work, but I don't think it is going to be that easy to do.

"You don't have shit to say, Sameria?" Zion spat with an attitude.

"I mean... I don't really know what to say," I admitted, twiddling my fingers.

"Don't act like you just innocent in all this. You know I saw that nigga Ro, right? You back fucking with him? That's why you actin' like this and trying to play me like I'm just some hoe ass nigga?" Zion spat, standing up with his daughter in his arms, putting a card with my name on it on the table and storming off.

"Zion, wait!" I said and my momma rushed over to me.

"Don't go chasing after no nigga. Especially not him, fuck him! Go around and talk to these people. All the fucking money me and Joy done spent on this party. You done spent half the damn party chasing niggas around," my momma whispered loud enough for only me to hear, then rushed away and went back to being fake with more than half of the people in this damn backyard.

I just wanted everybody to leave, so I can go to sleep. My head was pounding and I just wanted to go in the house, get in the shower and get in my bed. I can't believe that Zion went off and then just left before I could even respond to the shit that he was accusing me of that wasn't even true. Then again, a part of me is happy that he left because that will make it easier to start getting over him now. Tears started to burn my eyes, but I fought them back as Cina and Unique rushed over to me.

A few hours passed by and everybody stared leaving. I

don't know who was happier, me or my momma. Cina and Unique stayed to help us clean up. The whole time, all my momma did was talk shit about my dad's sisters and his mom. I still don't understand why she invited them here today. She didn't invite them to my graduation.

"That's wrong, you can't make the decisions for her for the rest of her life. She's about to go off to college and you're not going to be able to dictate what she does and who she does it with. You doin' bullshit like this is the reason she doesn't tell yo' ass shit. You just pushing her away more and more, Susie!" Joy said, catching me and Cina's attention.

"You raise your daughter however the fuck you choose, but Sameria is my daughter, and I know what's best for her. You can have an opinion, but if you know what's best for you, you'll keep it to yo' damn self when it comes to my kids!" My momma spat.

"Why are y'all tripping. Y'all need to calm down," I said, trying to get them to calm down and just talk things out.

"That's it, I'm done with you. You just want them to be lonely and miserable just like you!" Joy said and made her way into the house with my momma on her heels.

I've never seen them like this before. They talk shit to each other and never hold back what's on their mind, but it's never got heated like this. My momma always says that real friends don't argue with each other, but they'll have yo' back and go toe to toe with other bitches when it comes to you. I don't even know what to say because I can't believe that this is even happening.

"Yea, bitch, you're miserable and you're a liar. Tell them the fucking truth! I been putting up with yo' shit for

years because I considered you my friend. I never turned
my back on you even when I knew that I should have.
The only reason why I even stayed friends with you was
so I could still be in Sameria's life but bitch, today is the
day I'm done with yo' ass," Joy said as she gathered her
shit and made her way to the door.

"Joy, wait!" I screamed out.

"Don't say that bitch name ever again in this house,
and I wish you would think about running after her. I'll
drag you by the ponytail back in this house!" My momma
spat and just stared at me, waiting for me to make the
wrong move.

I made my way over to the window and watched Joy
pull out the driveway. Tears that I had been holding back
for half the party started to fall down my face. Some were
for Joy, thinking about the fact that somebody that has
loved me, supported me and had my back through everything is gone just that fast. When my momma couldn't
show up to programs, award ceremonies and anything
else that involved me, Joy made sure that she was there.

Then there was the fact that today is the last day that I
would get to see or talk to Zion. The one problem that I
had with him, he fixed, and I listened to my momma and
let him leave. Just like I just did with Momma Joy. I didn't
even look at my momma or say anything to her. I made
my way upstairs, so I could pack the rest of my shit. I can't
wait to get the fuck out of this house.

"I don't give a fuck how mad you are. You better bring
yo' ass back down here and finish getting this house back
together. I'm going to take a nap, so I can go to work at
midnight. Before I get back to this house, it better be
spotless or that's yo' ass!" My momma yelled up the stairs.

14

SCAR

"R'Shad!" Pumpkin screamed as I got out the rental.

My auntie was so damn loud, I know that everybody on the block can hear her ass.

"Whose fucking car is that? Did you fuckin' steal it? Don't fucking lie to me either, nigga!" Pumpkin spat so damn fast once I got in front of her.

"Pumpkin, I don't steal cars," I said as I walked by her and in the house.

She followed behind me like I knew she would. She needs to be worried about Ricardo and that shit he's driving. When I came home, my little brother was getting money, and he introduced me to the game. Pumpkin knows what we do, that's my nigga, I tell her everything. In a short amount of time, I'd been able to get a bag and shit been going smooth. Every other day, I'm in a different rental car, and she already knows wassup. All she asks is that we don't have the police running up in her house, and I'm always sure that I don't do that.

I flopped down on the couch as my brother came into the house. I could hear Cina and loud ass Sameria talking outside. Sameria always got a fucking attitude; the bitch can't ever just be happy. She gets on my fuckin' nerves. Every time she comes around, she got some smart-ass shit to say.

My brother and I discussed some moves that we needed to make today, some shit on the floor for some more money. That reminded me, I got a few people that owe me some money. It's going to be fucking payday today.. This bitch Lexi owes me some money, and I haven't been able to get up with her, but today, I'm going to go and find that bitch.

"Shut yo' big head ass up, damn!" I yelled as Sameria walked in the house.

"R'Shad, you shut the fuck up,'" Sameria said, rolling her eyes.

"I thought you were leaving for college. Damn! When? So, I can fucking celebrate. I thought that once they moved, I would never have to see yo' ass again, but every time they come over, here yo' ass come," I spat.

"I leave next week and don't worry, I won't miss yo' rude ass either," Sameria said. She picked up an empty ashtray and tried to throw it in my face, but I blocked it.

"You are fucking lucky that didn't hit me in my face. Get the fuck out! Cina, go visit her at her house," I spat, meaning every word.

"Sameria, I like you. You cool, but you throw something else in my house, I'll break yo' fuckin' hand," Pumpkin said, serious as hell.

"My bad, P," Sameria replied.

"Y'all need to just get together and quit playing," Pumpkin said and everybody except Sameria and I cosigned.

"Her mouth too smart, I be done caught a fucking case," I replied.

Sameria didn't say anything, she just kept mugging me. They all think that shit is funny because they stay bringing up that we should fuck with each other. I got a bitch, and I'm good where I'm at. We all sat and kicked it for a few hours, trying to let it cool down some outside.

"Come with us to the park right quick," Ricardo said.

We all made our way outside and Pumpkin followed to go back on the porch with her friends. It's hot as hell. I'm surprised she sittin' out here. I handed Pumpkin some money as I walked by and kissed her on the cheek. Ricardo and me always make sure Pumpkin is good. If I got to go and take it from another nigga, she's going to always be good. I'll do anything for P.

"Be careful," Pumpkin said as we walked away.

Every time I leave the house, she says that shit. I know that she be worried about us, but I'm going to always be good. I got my brother back and he got mine. I'm not going back to jail and I'm going to get a muthafucka before they ever get me. We made it around the corner to the park and everybody was out here.

Ricardo lit his blunt as we got out the car and finished talking about the business we couldn't discuss in Pumpkin's house with her listening. Antonio walked up on us and hopped his ass right in rotation, hitting the fuck out of Ricardo's blunt, smelling like cheap ass liquor. He's been getting shit together, so he can get back into the business, but I know he not ready yet. My phone started ringing and it was Felicia. I let it keep ringing. I don't feel like arguing right now. My mind is on getting some money, I'll call her back later.

"Y'all see that nigga, Sevino, over there. That nigga really getting money. All he fucks with is bad bitches and you see that truck that nigga driving. I'm gon' get me one of them bitches real soon!" Antonio said, moving his hands, motioning for us to look at the nigga Sevino.

"Nigga, damn, is you one of his bitches?" Ricardo asked.

"Get off that nigga dick. Quit acting like a bitch. Why the fuck you worried about what is on another nigga table if you ain't sitting at it?" I said, shaking my head.

We sat at the park chilling for a few hours. I looked over at Sevino, but I noticed Lexi's big booty ass all in his face. Even though her back is turned to me, that ass is one of a kind and that's that hoe. This bitch out here tricking with niggas, she better have my fucking money. I'm not in the business of getting' bitches high for free. Ricardo noticed me looking in Lexi's direction.

When I was locked up, Sevino's little brother, Meezy, looked out on several occasions. When I first got locked up, several niggas tried me, trying to take my food and shit, treating me like some bitch ass nigga. In the beginning, I was fighting every fucking day. Meezy had my back from day one. When I fought, he fought and vice versa. Our bond got so tight that even right now if that nigga ever needed anything, I would always be there for him.

Meezy tried to get me down with Sevino and his crew

when I came home, but he kept saying that I wasn't ready yet. Ricardo was fucking with this nigga named Block moving his work until he got locked up. He fucked with his wife, but she moved and ever since, he's been forced to sale some bullshit. Being able to touch the work that Sevino putting out would be what we need, but I'm not begging no nigga for shit. As I got lost in my thoughts, I came up with a plan. I know that my brother got me with whatever, so I decided to make my move to get us on all the way.

"Send Sameria and Cina to the store," I whispered to Ricardo.

Chaos shook his head and handed Cina some money to go to the store, giving her a long ass list of shit to get. If she remembers half that shit, she got a good ass memory because that nigga just naming shit trying to get her out the way. Cina and Sameria made their way to the car. Once we couldn't see them anymore, it was time to put my plan in motion. One thing that is going to make this shit work is the fact that Ricardo may be quiet, but that nigga is just as crazy as me.

I looked over at Ricardo, and I shook my head. With Ricardo at my side, we made it over to them and I saw this nigga looking real suspicious watching Sevino. Lexi better have my fucking money in that big ass purse. I hit the nigga in the head with one bullet that was creeping up on Sevino. Two niggas sitting back leaning against a black Impala started bustin' in our direction. One by one, my brother hit them niggas.

"Bitch, give me my muthafuckin' money!" I spat.

Every bitch in the park was running and screaming

but her and that's how I know this bitch was setting this nigga Sevino up. She was moving to slow for me. I snatched her purse, got my money out of it and threw it at her feet. I took exactly what she owed me and nothing more. Sevino punched her to the ground and some other niggas ran over, snatching her up off the ground. I could hear the fucking police sirens, and they weren't far away.

Ricardo and I hauled ass back to my rental. He got on the phone telling Cina to go to Pumpkin's and to not go back to the park. That nigga Sevino thought I wasn't ready before, but I know that he knows I am now. Ricardo lit another blunt and skirted away from the curb. This nigga needs to go to rehab. All he does is smoke weed.

"R'SHAD! SOMEBODY IS HERE FOR YOU!" Pumpkin screamed from the living room.

I just went to sleep and here she goes lettin' muthafuckas in the house. I checked my phone and it was nine in the morning. I'm going to have to hear Felicia's mouth because I didn't come by her house, but shit, I was tired. She done called my ass like 20 fucking times. After my brother and I handled some business, I ended up coming back here and got dressed to go see her but ended up falling asleep.

I got up and looked out the window. I saw that nigga Sevino's truck outside. I went to the bathroom to brush my teeth and get myself together. I slipped my pole in my pants and made my way downstairs. Ricardo was already sitting in the living room.

"Scar, right?" Sevino asked, and I nodded my head as I sat down.

Pumpkin made her way out the living room. Somebody called and tried to tell her about what happened at the park as I was coming in the house last night, and she cussed them out, but she didn't ask me no questions. She knows me, and she knows that I don't give a fuck and will set it the fuck off with no problem. Pumpkin also knows that Ricardo is going to ride with me with whatever I do and that it how it has always been.

"I appreciate what y'all did yester—" Sevino attempted to say as Antonio came stumbling in the room.

A drunk ain't shit. I just looked over at my brother and that let him know that I'm not fucking with his cousin. I could hear Pumpkin talking shit outside on the porch. How the fuck you supposed to be getting money if you always drunk? A nigga could run up on you and do anything to yo' ass, and you wouldn't even see it coming. I shook my head as this drunk ass nigga jumped on this nigga Sevino's dick like he was yesterday.

"My man, can I finish talking to them and then I'll get with you?" Sevino said, trying to get Antonio's drunk ass out of his face.

Antonio, holding on to the wall, made his way out the room. His ass was struggling to get up the stairs from how the fuck it's sounding. It sounds like that nigga 'bout to tumble down the fucking stairs. I'm sick of him. When Pumpkin kicked him out, he left and got it together for a few days. I told Pumpkin and Ricardo that shit wasn't gon' last and look, I was fucking right.

I'm gon' have to get my own spot sooner than later. Pumpkin doesn't want me to leave, but her son is getting

on my damn nerves. I'm not about to deal with this shit
every day. Having to tell him to leave the first-time hurt
Pumpkin, and I don't think that she could do it again. I'm
stepping to that nigga today and letting him know what it
is. If I move out, I can't be worried about what the fuck he
doing and how the fuck it could come back on Pumpkin.

After we fought, we didn't see each other for some
time. Pumpkin tried to get us to talk, but I didn't have shit
to say that was going to be nice, so out of respect for
Pumpkin, I just kept my distance from him. I stayed in
the streets and at Felicia's a lot, so we hardly ever saw
each other. Whenever we do, this nigga makes me want
to beat his ass again, but that ain't gon' do shit, that nigga
ain't gon' ever change. Ricardo and I usually agree on
damn near everything, but him insisting on keeping this
nigga in our business is some shit that I'm losing all my
patience with. That nigga is a liability and causing too
many fucking problems, family or not!

"Back to what I was saying. Y'all came through
yesterday and for that, I got a position at my table,"
Sevino said.

"What's the position?" I asked as soon as the last word
left his mouth.

A nigga will tell you anything and I'll never let
anybody try to do no fuck shit involving me and my
brother. We ain't starving, but more money wouldn't be a
fucking problem either. I'm not about to just agree to
some shit because of who he is. His name holds weight,
but it's going to take more than that to fucking impress
me. He knows that he needs us and that is why he is
sitting in my fucking living room.

"Nigga, I like you. Yo' ass is crazy, but that's that shit

that I need on my team. You not like some of these clown ass niggas out here. I know I told Meezy before y'all wasn't ready, but y'all showed me yesterday that y'all ready now," Sevino said as he went on to tell us about the position.

"We will be in touch," I said as my brother and I jumped up at the same time from the couch.

"Talk to you two soon," Sevino said, using emphasis on *two*, letting me know Antonio wasn't included in the offer.

Sevino made his way out to the porch, talking to Pumpkin and her questioning him. Pumpkin is crazy, and you never know what might come out of her mouth, but she always got our back no matter what. My brother and I made our way to the kitchen to talk. That's our spot to talk. It's a habit we started when we were kids, so nobody could hear us, and it stuck throughout the years.

"What you think about working for him?" Ricardo asked.

"I'm not working for no muthafuckin' body. We can work with him and sit at the table like he said, or we can get the fuck on until we come across something better or just as good," I spat.

Ricardo nodded his head, agreeing with me. I know my brother better than anybody, so I know that when he's quiet, that nigga is plotting. A lot of muthafuckas think because he's usually quiet that they can try him, but it doesn't take long for them to realize that he quiet, but that nigga crazy. The loudest nigga is usually the weakest and the quiet one is the nigga that you need to watch. We agreed to make Sevino wait, that way he will come back with a better deal the next time around.

I made my way to my room to pick out my clothes for today. With what I know we will have coming in soon, it's time to make some more moves in the street to make sure that we can hold down what we have and take over what we need. I turned on the shower to get it hot and made my way into my room to pick out my fit for the day and get my du-rag to keep my waves right.

"Yo' ass got ocd like my sister, I swear," Pumpkin said, standing in my doorway.

"I know just like her and shit, being locked up just made it worse. Some of them niggas was so trifling," I replied.

My momma didn't play no games about making sure our house was in order. While my brother is messy as hell, I always made sure my clothes were folded neatly and all my shit was ironed before I put it onhangers. My room is spotless, and everything is in its place. I decided on a pair of True Religion jeans with a matching red and white shirt. I took out a pair of my white high-top air force one's. I got five pairs of the same damn shoe and if I put a crease on one of them, I make sure to replace them.

"R'Shad, please be careful if you are going to fuck with that nigga Sevino, and look out for Ricardo," Pumpkin said as she came into my room.

"Pumpkin, I got us no matter what. You already know that," I said as I dapped up my gangsta ass auntie.

"Did Felicia move?" Pumpkin asked me.

"Yea. Why?" I asked.

"Shit, that's what I want to know. Why she move?" Pumpkin said, shrugging her shoulders and making her way out of my room.

"P, will you just give her a chance? Damn, you be trippin' on her, but you don't even really know her like that," I said.

"I know enough. I know that my sister didn't like the bitch and that's all that I need to know!" Pumpkin spat and made her way downstairs.

15

CHAOS

"Ricardo, I can tell by the look in yo' eyes that you are about to go out and do some bullshit," Pumpkin said as she came downstairs.

"Pumpkin, I'm good. I got this and us no matter what, you know that."

"You need to be worried about Cina and your daughter," Pumpkin said as she followed me into the living room lighting a cigarette.

"With everything I'm doing, I always make sure they are going to be good, Pumpkin. You know how I feel about Cina and my baby."

Pumpkin didn't say anything because she already knows how I feel when it comes to them. Pumpkin, just like Cina, feels that I give too much to the streets and I'll never get it back, but instead, I miss time with them. Cina is my heart and I'll do anything to make sure that she is always good. Right now, that means that I have to be away from them, but later on, shit will be different, and it will be worth it.

When all a nigga had was money to get her hair and nails done, she stood by me. Before she got pregnant, Cina was right with me in the trap, cooking and bagging up work. For her loyalty and love, I will always be with Cina and as soon as my money is all the way right, I'm going to give her a ring.

Making us more of a necessity for Sevino, my brother and I came up with a plan to take over some spots that's booming. They can either take our work and give us a cut, or they'll end up on the ten o'clock news. We decided to split up to get more work done. We sat and talked with Pumpkin throwing in her opinions for a few hours. Antonio must be sobering up because he finally made his way downstairs. I would take him with me but in his current state, he would just be in the way.

"Damn, when you get that?" Antonio asked, pointing to my watch with his free hand and holding a plate of food in the other.

"The other day."

If this nigga wasn't paying for pussy, he could have one and some more shit. As he looked up and down at my five-hundred-dollar True Religion jeans and matching green shirt with my low-top Air force one's, I could tell that he felt a way, but I pushed that to the back of my head because he's family. My brother is here to look out for Pumpkin, but this nigga is here because he not ready to be on his own.

I made my way out as Pumpkin grabbed my arm. "Chaos, I'm calling ya yellow ass that because I know from the look in yo' eyes that is what you are about to go cause. Be safe and make it home to Cina."

The newspaper gave me that name from some

charges that I caught. That shit stuck and the hood started calling me that. I was able to get probation and as long as I don't do nothing that gets back to them and drop clean whenever they want me to, I'll stay free. I'll just use Scar's piss. One of these niggas out here ain't dumb enough to call the police. If one gets scared enough to, then them and all they people will have to face me.

"I am, Pumpkin."

"It is my job to make sure that you and R'Shad are always good. I owe my sister that and so much more. I'm going to always be on yo' ass, and don't you forget it," Pumpkin sternly said as she let go of my arm.

Ever since the morning when my father killed my mom, I changed. I went from playing football and being all about my promising future to turning cold. I stayed in school because of Pumpkin pressuring me to be the first man to graduate in our family. Even when I go to school, I do the bare minimum and I still keep a 3.9 gpa. I got one more year left, and I'll be done.

I hopped in my G whip and made my way to the first stop. R'Shad expanded his clientele to some people that have real money to spend. He finessed them into signing for his rental cars in exchange for product. My stolen cars have been doing me just fine so far. After a few days, I ditch them and go back to the other side of town to get another one. I told Cina that I would buy a car soon, so I'm just waiting for a call to pick up my box Chevy my nigga Chuck is working on.

Checking the time on my phone and looking at the picture on my lock screen of my momma, I reached under my seat to grab what I needed and made my way out the car. As I walked up on the nigga that is supposed to be guarding the trap, I snuck up on him. By the look in his face, he knew who I was, and I know that he was scared out of his mind. I smiled as I watched him stir in the plastic lawnchair he was sitting in.

"Where is Cash at?" I asked.

"I don't know. He ain't here," his brother, Rob, stuttered saying, so I know he's lying.

"So, he ain't in the house?" I asked.

I checked my surroundings and before this nigga could lie again, I met him with my pole and forced him out the chair. He didn't put up a fight, he just started begging for his life. "Save all that bullshit and walk, nigga!" I spat.

Once I got him on the closed in porch, I put the plastic that I brought with me over his head and let myself in the spot because these dumb muthafuckas left the door unlocked. Rob led the way with my pole pressed to his back and we came up on Cash and a bitch in the living room.

"What the fuck?" Cash spat as I had a seat across from him in the recliner, watching his brother gasping for air in the plastic that I tied tight around his head.

"The way I see it, you got one choice. You either take my shit and report to me, or I'll kill you and your brother," I said, making it plain and simple what the fuck it is.

"What do you want, money? I'll give you everything I got, just let me and my brother go," Cash's bitch ass pleaded.

"Send that bitch to go get it," I said, and the bitch jumped up on her own and made her way to the back of the house.

Cash jumped up trying to get to his brother. "Muthafuka, you might want to sit down!" I spat as I pointed my pole in his direction. From the look in his eyes, I could tell he was scared. As long as he does what I say when I say, there is no reason for him to worry about him. The bitch brought me the money, and I started to give Cash specific instructions on what he needed to do.

"If you don't do exactly what the fuck I said, I'm going to send somebody to take yo' bitch. Not for me because she a'ight, but she ain't fucking with what I got!" I spat as I jumped up to leave.

"What type of nigga would just sit and let a nigga come and take they shit? How the fuck can he just come in here and tell you what the fuck you gon' do and yo' punk ass just go with it? The last thing I need is a bitch ass nigga. I might as well get a fucking girlfriend. Nigga, I'm done with you, lose my fucking number!" The bitch went off as I made my way out.

I WAS SITTING at my cousin Yoni's hair shop, waiting for my barber to get there. Yoni's mom and my mom are first cousins. I hate coming here, but my shit was looking rough, so I had to come today. Yoni and Cina been talking since we got in here about an hour ago. R'Shad was on his way so we could talk about where we are at with getting shit done. I handled my part and now we just have to wait for Sevino to pop up again. Hopefully he handled his side, so we'll be ready for whatever comes next.

"What's up, Chaos?" This bitch named Mia asked as she walked in the shop.

"Bitch, ain't shit up with him. Yo' best bet will be to keep it moving before you get beat the fuck up!" Cina yelled as she jumped up fast as fuck like she ain't big as hell and pregnant.

"Bitch, I'm not interested, and you already know that!" I spat, causing the smile that spread over Mia's face to disappear.

"Cina, sit the fuck down," I said as calmly as I could.

Mia made her way over to Jazzy's chair and plopped down looking embarrassed. Cina hesitated but when I gave her a fucking look, she sat her ass down. Cina is so damn fine when she's mad. Her chocolate skin started glowing more and the way she was mugging Mia, I wanted to laugh so bad. Mia, to the average nigga, would be a bad bitch that you would want to fuck, but I know what I got with Cina. No bitch is worth fucking up shit with my family.

I looked back over at Cina, and she was mugging me still and got a fucking attitude now. I got up, grabbed Cina by her arm and pulled her over to me. Sitting back in Yoni's chair with Cina on my lap, I started rubbing her stomach. I can't wait for my baby to get here.

"I don't know why you let these bitches get to you, Cina. You know how Chaos is when it comes to you. He don't want none of these bitches," Yoni confirmed what everybody already knew.

"Nigga, we got a problem with yo' fuckin' cousin, bra. I keep telling you about this nigga!" R'Shad spat as he walked into the shop.

I thought that I was going to be able to go home and

spend time with Cina, but that is out the fucking question. I already know that Antonio done got himself in some shit that me and R'Shad have to get him out of. It's always something with this nigga, and we're going to have to sit down with him and go over the changes that are about to happen. If he wants to continue to be a part of this business with us, he is going to have to get his shit together for real this time and not just for a few days.

"That means you about to be gone all night because of you and that *he's family* shit," Cina said, snatching away from my grasp and jumping out of my lap.

Cina wobbled away and made her way to the back of the shop. Cina has been working here after school and on the weekends. I know that with her getting further along she wants me around more. Shit, I want to be around more, but the bills have to be paid. She already knows what it is, but because she in her feelings, I need to go and talk to her before I leave out.

"Nigga, go handle that and meet me at Pumpkin's in an hour," R'Shad spat and made his way out the shop.

Yoni and I discussed some business for a few minutes. When I got up to go and check on Cina, two police officers walked into the shop, causing me to stop in my tracks. Yoni stopped what she was doing and made her way to the door. Unless they have a warrant, they won't be checking shit in here.

"I'm the owner of the shop. How can I help you?" Yoni asked with an attitude, folding her arms across her chest.

"We're looking for Cina Miller. Where is she?" The black officer asked with an attitude.

"What are you looking for her for?" I demanded to know and impatiently waited for a fucking answer.

"What's your name, buddy?" The white officer asked as his partner continued to scan the shop.

"You're looking for Cina, what the fuck do you need to know my name for?" I spat, losing my patience.

"So, you don't want to give up your name, huh? Well can you read?" The black officer questioned, getting close enough to me that I know I'm going to jail while handing me some papers.

"We are looking for Cina Miller like my partner here has already stated. She has been reported as a runaway. Her mother gave this address as one of the possible places that we may be able to find her. We also have a warrant for you, Ricardo," the white officer said as he snatched the warrant out of my hand, threw it to the ground and swiftly jerked both of my arms behind my back.

"What the fuck are you arresting him for?" Yoni screamed as she pulled out her phone.

"You're the owner, right? Then I suggest you read the warrant if you have any questions," the officer said.

"You can answer my fucking question! This is my cousin, and he's a minor!" Yoni screamed as Cina came into the room.

"Are you Cina Miller?" The officer asked as I looked up at Cina and tears filled her eyes.

"What the fuck are you doing? Why the fuck are you arresting him?" Cina cried as one of the officers ushered me out the shop.

"Cina, don't trip. I'm good. We gone be good. I got us," I vowed before the shop door closed behind me.

Hearing Cina's cries just made me feel even worse than I already did. I damn sure didn't see this coming.

Yoni came running out the shop and from behind me she let me know that Pumpkin was coming to get me. The officer kept telling her to stop talking to me and to go back in the shop, but her ass ain't trying to hear that. Yoni don't give a fuck, and she not gon' stop until she's ready.

"Maybe, next time you'll keep yo' hands to yourself, tough guy," the officer commented and slammed the police car door.

What the fuck is this nigga talking about? I know them bitch ass niggas, Rob and Cash, didn't call twelve on me. All the shit that I've done here lately, who knows what the fuck this is about. With me being on probation, it doesn't take much for them to get a warrant.

16

CINA

"You need to come with us," the officer pleaded as I plopped down in my chair and buried my face into my hands.

"Your mom wants you home to ensure that you are safe. You have a baby that you need to worry about. Right now, it is best that you come with us." A woman that was dressed in regular clothes said as I looked up.

She introduced herself as Taniece. She explained that she is the social worker that has been assigned to my case. It never even crossed my mind that Rita would report me as a runaway. I've been gone for this long and it hasn't been an issue. All of a sudden, she wants to pretend to be concerned. I know what that bitch wants but discussing that shit with these people will just cause more problems.

"How are you, Cina? How are you feeling? How's the baby?" Taniece asked.

"How the fuck do you think I feel? Why are y'all

arresting him?" I screamed in-between trying to catch my breath from crying.

"Cina, it has been reported to us that Ricardo has been abusing you and holding you against your will. Your mother has filled a report, and we also have a witness who has already given a statement," Taniece pleaded and attempted to rub my back.

Snatching away from her and jumping up from the chair, I didn't have shit to say to her. I packed up all my supplies and Chaos and my pictures off my work station as tears continued to fall. Taniece was still talking and as far as I'm concerned, nothing that she is saying matters. The fact that they are trying to accuse Ricardo of holding me hostage and putting his hands on me is straight bull-shit. I would say that I am surprised, but with a mother like the one I got, anything is possible. All she cares about is making me suffer.

Hearing Taniece telling me how concerned Rita is with my wellbeing and how much she loves me, I wiped the tears that were falling and couldn't help but laugh because that is a joke. Rita cares about herself and Sin, but me, she damn sure doesn't care about me. If she cared, she would have been there way before today. What I want to know is who the fuck is this witness that they have because it damn sure can't be her. She can barely make it to the corner store sober, so testifying in court isn't going to happen. I don't know how this shit happened with these charges, but if I have anything to do with it, they won't stick.

"If y'all taking me home, then take me! I don't want to talk to you lady!" I demanded as I made my way to the door.

If I wasn't pregnant, I damn sure wouldn't walk out this bitch without a fight, but I have to think about my daughter. Taniece offered to help me with my bags, but I just continued to mug her. The last thing I need is her help. I texted Pumpkin, letting her know what was going on. Taniece led the way to her city car. My phone started ringing and it was Sameria. Not wanting Taniece in my business, I started texting Meria, letting her know what was going on, even though I'm sure somebody done ran they mouth and that is why she's calling right now because I just talked to her and she was getting her stuff ready for her to leave for college.

"Can I just go home now? How many times are you going to ask me the same questions? My answer is not going to change? Ricardo has never put his hands on me, and I wasn't being held hostage," I said, holding my stomach and just ready to get the fuck away from Taniece and her damn coworkers.

I'd been downtown for three hours. They claimed that Rita was coming to get me, but she ain't been here yet. As much as I can't stand her, I'd rather be with her right now than having to deal with these people. I know that they are just trying to get me to admit some shit that never happened between Ricardo and me to make their job easier.

"Okay, we'll be right out," Taniece said into the phone.

"I just have one more question and then you can go. Your mother is waiting in the lobby for you. I need to know if you know anything about Ricardo selling drugs?" Taniece said, damn near begging at this point.

"Ricardo doesn't sell drugs. He goes to school and is on the football team."

"Sweetie, you're going to learn the hard way that trying to cover for that boy isn't going to get you anywhere. You need to be more focused on yourself and your daughter. What kind of future are you going to have living life the way that you do? Have you thought about the way that your actions can impact your daughter's life? How are you going to look your daughter in the eyes one day and explain to her that her father is dead or in prison?" Taniece questioned.

"My future is going to be just fine, and so will Ricardo's. You need to be more concerned with checking on Monae!" I spat, throwing Monae Williams' file into her face, causing all the papers to fall out and scatter all over her desk.

I know Monae, and I know that somebody really needs to check on her. Not only is her momma kicking her ass, everybody in the neighborhood knows that her momma is fucking with that man that is a fucking predator. Why they worried about me and I'm perfectly fine? They need to be investigating the muthafuckas that need to be investigated. I made my way to the lobby and found Rita talking to the secretary, tapping her foot.

Turning to face me, she jogged in my direction and then wrapped her arms around me. The smell of stale cigarettes, weed and my Japanese Cherry Blossom mist that I know Rita took as soon as I left her house the last time was making me nauseous. The show that she was putting on for these people is crazy. She even got the nerve to be making some fake ass tears come down her face.

"I'm so happy that they found you, baby," Rita lied like it was nothing, still holding me tight.

I couldn't help but roll my eyes. This shit is a joke and if I know my momma like I do, this is all a plan for her to get something that she doesn't have to work for. My momma is the type of woman that goes around to charities and churches every month with a sob story getting donations and any damn thing else that they are giving away just because she can. She's the type of person that will take anything even if she doesn't need it, just being greedy and taking away from people that really need help.

"Ms. Miller, here are the numbers you asked for and bus passes. Also, here are the gift cards, so that you're able to get groceries and other household items that you need. If you need anything, don't hesitate to give me a call," Taniece said, catching Rita's attention and causing her to let go of me to turn to face her.

Rita didn't hesitate in snatching the papers and the gift cards from Taniece's hand. In Taniece's mind, I'm sure that she thinks that she is doing her job and providing assistance to a poor, single, mother of two. The reality is that to my momma, this is just another scam. She will comply with these people to get all that she can out of them and then she'll be onto the next.

"Thank you. Thank you so much. I need to get my baby home, so I can make sure that her and my grandbaby are good and safe," Rita said, getting anxious to hit a cigarette and get away from these people.

Rita and I made our way to the elevator. If she was

really concerned, she would have offered to take my backpack or one of the other bags that I'm carrying, but she didn't. I couldn't help but roll my eyes behind her back as she spoke to every person that we passed by. This the type of fraudulent shit she does, so I'm not even surprised by what the fuck I just saw. I checked my phone to see if Pumpkin responded to my message, but she hasn't.

Rita and I stepped onto the elevator and the whole ride down was quiet and awkward as hell. The look that my momma was giving me said everything that needed to be said with no words being uttered between us. I couldn't stop thinking about Ricardo and silently prayed he is okay and that they release him today. I know that running away is just going to cause more problems that I don't need. Not only for me, but Ricardo too. I would feel a little better if I just knew that Ricardo was okay.

We finally made it to the first floor, still not saying shit to each other. Stepping off, I saw Pumpkin coming through the metal detectors. Stopping in my tracks, everything in me wanted to just walk off and follow Pumpkin. Pumpkin looked at up as she was being wanded by one of the security guards and mugged the fuck out of me and my momma.

"Look, see how that bitch is looking at you. And that's where you thought you wanted to be. They don't give a fuck about yo' ass," Rita whispered, looking at me over her shoulder.

"Aye! Aye! Cina, give me my keys!" Pumpkin screamed from behind me, causing me to stop.

I took off my backpack and went through it looking for my keyring. I found it and went to take Pumpkin's keys off it but before I could, Pumpkin snatched the entire keychain out of my hand. Rita didn't even notice that I wasn't walking behind her anymore, and she made her way out the front door of the building.

"P! I need that, so I can get my stuff out the house," I said, so confused on why Pumpkin is tripping with me.

"If it's up to me, yo' ass won't get shit out that house," Pumpkin reassured me.

"Keep the shit in the house. I promise she gone get so much more, and I'm going to make sure of it. Bitch!" Rita spat from behind me, grabbing me by my arm.

I snatched away from Rita and she looked at me with so much disgust. I know my momma and the type of person she is. I know the only thing that stopped her from putting her hands on me right now was the fact that there were too many witnesses around that could fuck up whatever bullshit she has in motion. We made it outside and looked around the lot for a familiar car. I just want to get to Rita's and get to my room. A horn honked, catching my attention. Looking in the direction of the horn, I saw Lil Miller behind the wheel of a White Impala.

I walked as fast as I could over to the car. The tears that I had been holding back just started to fall. I don't care about none of my shit that is in the townhouse. All I want is my daughter's stuff. My ultrasounds, scrapbooks and shit that I can't replace. I know how hard Pumpkin goes for her nephews and even though she didn't say it out her mouth, with the way she just handled me, she blames me for this happening. Pumpkin knows the situation with my mom. She also knows how I feel about Ricardo, so her thinking that I would have anything to do with what is going on, I just can't believe. When I got in the car, I didn't even waste my time speaking to Lil Miller. I don't have shit to say to his dusty, broke ass. Only Rita would think that it would be a good idea to come down-town with this nigga that is on the run.

"You thought those muthafuckas really gave a fuck about you. Look how that bitch just did you. You think that those muthafuckas are the world, but I got some-thing for all them bitches doe!" Rita said, meaning every word as she took a pull from a cigarette.

"Damn, you done got big, cuz," Lil Miller said while looking at me in the rearview mirror.

"I'm about to get the police to go with you to Pump-kin's to get all yo' shit. And you better get everything, I'm talking 'bout shit that ain't yours. All that new shit that I know that nigga been buying you and the baby. Get some of his shit too and you taking everything out that fucking townhouse. I know he got a bunch of new shit wit' the tags still on it," Rita said, and I could hear the excitement in her voice as Lil Miller's broke ass cosigned.

"I'm not going nowhere with the police," I replied.

"Oh, yo' black ass is going to go wherever the fuck I tell you to. And yo' black ass is going to do whatever the fuck I tell you to. You can't legally leave my house until you're eighteen, was the way that the judge explained it to me. Which means that I make the muthafuckin' decisions for you and yo' baby, little ungrateful bitch!" Rita spat.

When I was at Taniece's office, she told me that Sincere was the witness. He told them that he saw Ricardo beating me up at the park yesterday. I'm not mad at him because I know Rita made him do it. She must be desperate if she's involving her baby in this shit. We have to go to court in three days. I don't give a fuck what anybody says, I'm not lying to get Ricardo a fucking charge. My momma doesn't understand why I care about Ricardo the way that I do and let her tell it, he doesn't give a fuck about me.

"What you know about that nigga, Scar?" Lil Miller asked, staring at me in the rearview mirror.

From the dark circles and bags under his eyes, I know that he'd been poppin' perks bad. It looks like this nigga been up for days. If this nigga had any hustle to him, he could get money with his dad, my uncle Miller. My uncle can't stand my momma and doesn't fuck with Lil Miller because he's such a clown and a disgrace to his last name. There is no reason for Miller to be out here plotting on a come up. This nigga daddy is the man, but he too busy trying to fit in.

"I know you fucking heard him, bitch! Get to telling him what the fuck you know now or yo' baby will be wearing—" Rita attempted to say.

"I'm not telling him or you shii—" I started to reply before Rita turned around and smacked me so hard that I know her handprint is on my face.

17

SAMERIA

"Hey baby!" Joy screamed, happy to see me as I walked through her door.

"Hey," I replied dry as hell as Joy hugged me tight.

"So, you mad at me?" Joy asked as I plopped down on the couch.

"No. I already know how my momma is. I wish you could ride with us still. I have to be in the car with her for twelve hours, Momma Joy," I whined as Joy sat next to me and wrapped her arm around me.

It's been a little over two weeks since I saw Joy at my graduation party. We've talked on the phone and texted, but it's just not the same. She's had to work a lot lately, and we haven't been able to see each other. Being around her means a lot to me because she is such a big part of my life. Her and my mom tripping is some bull-shit, and I'll be happy when they makeup and get over it.

"Uhh, it's you," Tisha said as she came barging into the living room.

"Bitch, uhh to you and them dry ass braids!" I spat, not thinking twice.

"I don't know what the fuck either one of y'all problem is, but y'all need to cut that shit. Y'all are family and this shit needs to stop!" Joy demanded.

Tisha stormed back out the room faster than she came in. I didn't have shit to say about Tisha and my relationship. Tisha and I both used to be tight as fuck. We grew up together, but about a year ago is when shit went left. Tisha was trying to get with Chaos, but because she already knows how tight me and Cina are, she didn't want me to know. Chaos told me to tell her to leave him the fuck alone. She kept calling playing on his phone and passing letters through other people, but the bitch couldn't catch a clue. I told her that she needed to fall back and that she already knew that he had a girl. She felt that regardless of the situation, I was supposed to ride for her and be on her side because of us being god-sisters. Tisha kept saying shit like I was taking Cina's side and being fake. Right is right and wrong is wrong.

She was dead ass wrong and she decided she wasn't fucking with me no more because of that, so I haven't said shit nice to the bitch since then. Momma Joy knows what it is, and she knows what happened. She tried to get us to talk several times and then she decided that she was going to let us figure it out. I was done with her ass for good when she decided to link up with Zion's baby momma, Nessa, and that Tay. Ow all of a sudden them her ne best friends.

"What's wrong? You don't want to leave Zion?" Momma Joy asked.

"Naw, that's not it. I haven't talked to him, and I'm not

tripping. He made his decision, so it is what it is. I'm not
about to chase no nigga, that just ain't me," I replied, but
my heart had been saying something totally different.

"I know you and yo' ass is lying. You let yo' momma
make every decision for you. She picked that college. She
picked your major. She probably picked out that ugly ass
dress you got on too," Momma Joy said as I laid my head
on her shoulder.

"Will you tell me now?" I asked, trying to change the
subject.

"I already told you. I'll probably never talk to Susie
again, but it's not my place to tell you that. I'll never give
the bitch anything else, but I'd never do her like that. You
know me and it's damn near nothing that I won't do for
you. I love you just like I love Tisha, but I can't do that,
even to her," Joy replied, meaning every word.

"She's not going to tell me nothing and you already
know how she gets. I just came to say bye because we are
leaving early in the morning," I mumbled, scrolling
through Facebook.

My momma does dictate damn near everything in my
life. That is one reason I can't wait to leave for college, but
that ride is going to be a long one. I plan on sleeping for
most of it because I don't want to have to do no extra
talking to her. Since her and Joy fell out, she's been even
more distant than she normally is. Joy is her only friend,
so I know that she misses her, but she'll never admit it.
Knowing my momma, even if she is wrong, she'll never
admit that either. I'm riding with Momma Joy even
though I don't know what happened.

I've been begging Joy since my party to tell me what
her and my momma were arguing about and what was

she talking about, but every time she refuses. This time, she just gave me her reason. Shit, if she's never going to talk to my mom again, I don't see what the problem is and why she can't just tell me. I'll never find out what the fuck happened if it's up to my momma, so I'm not even going to waste my time with asking her.

My phone started ringing. Is my aunt Mikki, my dad's sister. When she came to my party, I was surprised because I hadn't seen them since my dad's funeral. They have never come around, and I never understood why. We exchanged numbers, and we've been texting here and there. I haven't told my momma because if she knew that I was talking to any of my dad's family, it would be a problem.

"Hey, what's up, Mikki?" I asked as I answered the phone.

"We got some stuff together for you. I wanted to see if we could meet up, so I can give it to you. I know yo' momma don't really like us, so I didn't know if I should stop by," Mikki replied laughing, but serious as hell.

"She at work. You can meet me at the house in like thirty minutes."

"Alright, I'm on my way. You want to run and get something to eat? And momma want see you before you leave too."

"Yea, we can do that." I hesitated, but I got a few more hours before Tasia gets out of cheerleading practice.

Mikki and I talked for a few minutes and then I ended the call. I always wondered why my dad's family never fucked with me, but I never asked. They don't live far from us, and they've never reached out or even made an attempt to. I would see them in passing or at the corner store here and there; they would speak but that was it ever since my dad was killed. My momma always told me that I didn't need them, I had her and that has always been my attitude. Besides Momma Joy, I never thought I needed no other family.

"Does Susie know that you talking to Mikki?" Momma Joy asked.

"Naw," I said, jumping up, so I could go and get myself together.

"I know she don't. Be careful. Don't ask no questions if you ain't ready for the answer," Momma Joy said as she hugged me tight and kissed me on the forehead.

"Okay. I love you, and I'll call you when I get down there."

"I love you too, and I'm going to miss you. You better call me and let me know that y'all made it down there too. If you need anything, I don't care what it is, you better call me. Don't get down there, meet a new nigga, fall in love and then start acting funny," Momma Joy said, hugging me and slipping an envelope in my purse.

As Momma Joy hugged me tighter and kissed me again, I could feel her tears wetting up the side of my face. She's been here through everything and has always had my back. I can't depend on many people, but I know that no matter what, Momma Joy and her husband will always come through. I hardly ever see my God dad Maurice because he's always at work, but when I need them, I can depend on them to come through.

As I made my way out of Joy's, I couldn't help but think about what she said about asking questions I'm not ready for the answer for. I don't have any expectations for my dad's family. I have a guard up when it comes to new people. My momma always talked so bad about these people when I was younger, honestly, I just been waiting for some bullshit to pop off.

"Momma, look who's here," Mikki said as we walked into my grandmother's home.

"Hi," I said with a fake ass smile, not really knowing what to say.

Cina is watching Tasia for me for a few hours while I spend some more time with my aunt. We went and got something to eat. I told her I would come to see my grandma, but I didn't know the whole family was going to be here. My mom is at home sleep, so I don't have to worry about her finding out where I'm at. I agreed to come over here, but I feel uncomfortable because I don't know what to expect. Mikki is cool, but I don't know nothing about the rest of these people.

"Come over here and give me a hug," my grandmother, Sharon, said, waving me over.

I made my way over to her and scanned the room, noticing a few people that came to my party and some people that I have seen in pictures from back in the day. Cousins, uncles and two more of my dad's sisters are all over here. I look just like my aunt Mikki. It's crazy that she's in her thirties, but she looks like she could be my age. Sharon patted on the couch next to her, trying to get me to sit next to her.

"Do she know what happened?" My aunt Terri tried to whisper across the room.

"All y'all get out. I want to talk to Sameria," Sharon said, catching everybody off guard.

"What do you mean get out?" My uncle Jigga asked, confused as hell.

"I don't repeat myself to my kids. Y'all all heard what I said," Sharon said, turning off the tv.

Everybody but Jigga caught the hint and got the fuck on. Jigga is the baby and from the look on his face, he damn sure ain't used to my grandma making him do something. I've seen him around a few times, but the crazy thing is that we knew who each other was but we never spoke. I remember Jigga coming around when I was younger a few times after my dad died and then all of a sudden, he just stopped.

"Jamar!" Sharon screamed.

"Momma, calm down, I'm leaving," Jigga said and then disappeared to the back of the house.

"You so pretty, but you got an attitude like yo' momma," Sharon said, trying to give me a compliment, but the shade was dripping from the last part.

"Thanks," I said, moving my hair from off my face and pulling it to the back.

"You got some long, thick, pretty, black hair. You got that from us because I ain't even gon' get started on yo' momma and em' hair. But I'm glad you came, it's been a long time. I don't want you to think that we don't love you because we do. We all do! Yo' momma didn't want us around you after my son, yo' daddy, was killed. It wasn't us. I tried several times to see you, and she wouldn't let me. I can't speak for nobody, but me. I just don't want you to go on with ya life and going off to college thinkin' we never wanted nothin' to do with you. Because she's yo' momma, I'm not gon' talk down on her right now with you sitting right here," Sharon said, staring into my eyes.

As Sharon kept talking, I searched her eyes for a lie, and I couldn't find one. Something is telling me that she isn't lying. As she was going on and on, laying everything out on the floor, I can't believe what I'm hearing. Momma Joy always told me to not go looking for shit that I wasn't ready to find and never ask a question if I ain't prepared for whatever the answer might be, but since she ain't holding shit back, I figure now is my opportunity.

"Who killed my dad?" I asked when Sharon stopped to take a sip of her coffee.

"You mean to tell me yo' momma never told you what happened to yo' dad?" Sharon asked, waiting for an answer.

"No, she won't talk about my dad," I admitted, silencing my phone once I saw that Zion was finally hitting my line.

"Momma, right now is not the time for this talk." Mikki said as she walked into the room.

"Didn't I tell you to get out?" Sharon asked, talking to Mikki but looking at me still.

Mikki didn't respond, she just made her way back out the room. I can't help but hear the rest of the family putting in their opinions about me and them wondering why I chose to come around now. I have no problem with telling them all what it is and before I leave, I'm going to make sure they all feel me, especially Jigga because he seems to have the most to say. He just in his feelings because his momma kicked him out the room for me.

"I ain't one to lie, so I'm going to make this plain for

you, baby girl, okay?" Sharon asked, waiting for an answer.

"Okay," I replied.

As my grandmother started to lay everything out that happened surrounding my father's death, I didn't know what to say. I started to interrupt several times, but every time, the words kept getting stuck in my throat. I started sweating, my throat started getting dry, and I started scratching my arms. When I'm uncomfortable, confused and distraught, the feeling that I'm feeling now comes over me. I'm taking in everything that she is saying to me, but I just can't believe that I'm hearing this shit.

Sharon and I finished talking. Well, she was doing all the talking and after about an hour, we made our way into the other living room where everybody else was at. I'm ready to go home, but who knows when I'll see them again. I was already looking at Jigga side-eyed because of the cold shoulder that he was giving, but I'm damn sure mugging him now. Sharon made her way out the room, leaving me alone with everybody else. My mind was running a mile a minute and I just couldn't stop thinking about all the shit that I just heard over and over in my head, trying to figure out how this happened.

"I'm about to go," I said as I stood up, tired of faking it. I needed to go and get Tasia and go home.

"What made you come over here all of a sudden?" Jigga asked, catching everybody's attention because they all stopped their side conversations.

"I came because Mikki told me that Sharon wanted to see me," I replied with all the attitude that I have dripping from my response.

"It sounds good," Jigga spat as he checked his phone.

"If you got something to say, gon' head and get it off yo' chest," I said, turning my whole body towards him, ready to get it poppin'.

"Little girl, I don't play with people kids. If I had something to say, then I would say it. You better take yo' ass back over there wit' yo' crazy ass momma," Jigga mumbled, causing me to jump up and leap in his direction.

"What the fuck is wrong with you? You can't talk about that girl momma. She ain't too damn crazy, you were fucking her, nigga!" Terri spat as Mikki grabbed me before I could get to Jigga.

When my grandmother told that part of the story that Jigga was messing with my mom, I started to think back to when Jigga used to always come around. It makes sense and his comment just shows that it for sure happened. Jigga didn't budge. He actually leaned back, damn near taunting me because he knew his sisters weren't going to let me get to him. He's a disrespectful ass nigga and the fact that he thought it was okay to say anything about my momma just shows how much of a bitch he is. Uncle or not, I'll never have any type of relationship with him.

I snatched away from Mikki and Gianni, one of our cousins, and made my way outside. No, I see why my momma kept me away from them. I wish I would have never seen Jigga, but I know that I needed to finally hear the truth about my dad's murder. I don't know how to feel. A part of me is mad, but then the other part is confused and still trying to wrap my head around everything that I was told. Mikki and Gianni are on my ass, and they followed me outside. I can hear my grandmother's weak voice calling out for me, but I don't think that I can take anymore of her revelations today.

"Sameria, wait," Mikki begged as I'd just started making my way down the street and pulling out my phone to call Momma Joy to come and get me.

I didn't respond to Mikki. I just kept walking down the street as my heart started pounding so fast like it was going to jump out of my chest. Momma Joy didn't answer, so I pulled up my Uber app to see how long it would take to get me a ride over here. Mikki caught up to me and tugged at my arm, causing me to stop in my tracks.

"Sameria, I came to yo' party when yo' momma sent the invitation to momma's because, like I told you, I wanted to get to know you. You're still my niece. I can't speak for everybody in the family, but we shouldn't have let it go on for so long. The shit that happened back in the day doesn't matter and has nothing to do with you. I know that Jigga is an asshole, and he was dead ass wrong for bringing up yo' momma. I know it's a lot to take in. We're family and can get through this together. I can take you home. You don't have to walk," Mikki pleaded, trying to get me to hear her out.

Checking my phone, for whatever reason, I saw it was a forty-five-minute wait for a car. I agreed that Mikki could take me home, but I don't have shit else to say right now to her or none of the rest of this family. I need some time to take all this in. I think about my dad all the time and with me leaving for college without him being able to be there, I've been thinking about him even more lately. No matter how I may feel about my momma and how she is, I would never let another muthafucka fix they mouth to say anything bad about her. My mom has so much pride and I always figured that was the reason she didn't ever ask for any help. I never thought that they offered to help and reached out to be a part of my life, and she refused to accept their help or even gave me the choice to get to know them. Talking to my momma about this now isn't going to get me anywhere. As Mikki drove me home, I just kept thinking about getting to Texas and being away from her too.

I said, goodbye to Mikki and got out of her car. Once she pulled off, I cut through the backyard and made my way over to Cina's, so I could get Tasia. My phone started ringing and checking the caller-id, it was Zion. I had been wanting him to call for weeks, but now it's too late. I don't have anything to say. With the headspace that I'm currently in, talking to him now isn't going to be good for either one of us. I slipped my phone back into my pocket.

Before I could knock on the door, Rita swung open the front door. Rita is so pretty, she has smooth chocolate skin just like Cina. Even with how old she is and all the drinking that she does, you could never look at her and guess her real age. Even wit' how fine and thick she is, under all that, she's still a miserable, lonely, old bitch. I complain a lot about my momma and how she is always trippin' about everything, but at least she ain't nothing like Rita.

"You done made yo' rounds to see all yo' niggas and got some dick?" Rita questioned and laughed.

"Naw, I was with my dad's people," I replied, keeping it short as I gathered all Tasia's stuff before going to get her from the back.

"I know Susie don't know that you were with them. I know damn well she ain't having that," Rita blurted out

and then threw up her hand and proceeded to dance as
Keith Sweat poured from speakers.

I didn't respond to her. Luckily, my momma won't
even speak to her, so I don't have to worry about her
telling my momma. She just nosy as hell. All her ass gon'
do is get on the phone with one of her sisters and gossip
about it. Rita is a trip and the older we get, the worse she
gets with all her bullshit. She needs to be worried about
the niggas in her driveway with Lil Miller. I made my way
to the back to Cina's room, and I doubt Rita's drunk ass
noticed right away.

"What's wrong with you, Meria?" Cina asked as I
walked in her room.

"Bitch, nothing," I lied and plopped down on her bed
next to Tasia who was knocked out snoring and all.

"Bitch, quit lying. I know you and in case you forgot,
you already know, bitch, ain't no secrets. You know every
damn thing about me, and I know every damn thing
about you, so get to talking, hoe," Cina demanded.

I started telling Cina everything that happened when
I was with Mikki, and I was just waiting for her to give
her damn two cents because she told me not to go over
there. She wasn't lying, we told each other everything. We
were always on the phone. Half the damn time, we would
be on the phone not even talking to each other for most
of the time, but let one of us try to hang up, it's a problem.
I'm going to miss Cina. Our lives are changing so much.
I'm leaving for school in a few hours, and she's back at
Rita's.

Chaos is in jail and the way that it seems things are
going, who knows when he's getting out. The most fucked
up thing is that they can't even talk to each other. The

prosecutor requested that a restraining order be put in place to keep Cina safe, which is bullshit. If anything, she was safer with Chaos than she is over at Rita's. It's killing Cina. I can tell from looking at her eyes, even though she's putting up a front, that she's been crying recently.

"Bitch, are you good?" I asked, already knowing the answer.

"No, the judge said today that I can't see Ricardo. They are talking about letting him out, but they made me leave the courtroom before they discussed any details. Rita thinks the shit is funny. She keeps talking shit and on top of that, Pumpkin won't talk to me," Cina finally replied and busted into tears.

"It's going to be okay, Cee. Chaos will be out, and you know that he's not going to let anything or anybody keep him away from you."

"What if it's not okay? If they do let him out and they find out that we have been talking to each other or been around each other, they'll just send him back to jail. What am I going to do, Meria? You're leaving, Chaos is gone, and I don't have anybody now," Cina pleaded as I hugged her tight.

I can't believe that Pumpkin is taking it this far. Chaos must not know because I know he wouldn't let that shit slide. Yoni came through a few days ago when I was here bringing stuff for the baby. Nobody fucks with Rita, but because they fuck with Chaos, I think eventually even Pumpkin will come around. I know that Pumpkin is stressed out because of Chaos being locked up, but she has to know that Cina had nothing to do with it.

"Did they let you talk today in court?" I asked.

"Yea, but shit, I feel like they weren't trying to hear

anything that I said. Rita didn't say shit, but she's said enough at all his other court dates. Because I'm a minor, they look at this shit like I'm in danger and all this shit can happen to me because Rita went in there lying, making up all types of shit. Telling the courts that Chaos was manipulating me, his entire family had me brainwashed and a bunch of other shit," Cina whined in-between crying.

I sat with Cina as we talked about everything, and she showed me pictures of the nails that she did today. My bestie is talented as fuck, and I know that all the dreams that she has about owning several shops and getting clientele booming is going to come. I can't wait for everything to fall in place for her. It seems that when things started to turn around and everything was going how she wanted to, a bunch of bullshit went down, dragging her back to her starting point all over again.

"What's up, Sameria?" Lil Miller asked, standing in the doorway of Cina's room.

"What's up?" I replied as I woke up Tasia, so we could get to the house.

Lil Miller has shot his shot several times and each time he gets turned down. He's such a clown and I would never fuck with a nigga like him. He just tries so damn hard to be in that street shit. He doesn't fit in at all and everybody can see it. He used to be cute, but them percocets done fucked him up bad, and he look old as hell to be my age. That nigga looks like that Mo Mo bitch. Lil Miller keeps trying to have small talk and he so damn high, he ain't even noticed that I'm not even responding.

"Bitch, I know you have to go, but you about to talk to me while you walk home," Cina whined.

"You so damn irritating. You a big ass baby," I said as Tasia clinged to me like I'm about to carry her big ass.

"So, what? Bitch, I'm calling yo' phone, so answer," Cina said like we weren't still standing in the same room.

"I can take y'all home," Lil Miller said as I turned to face him.

His eyes were barely open, and this nigga was damn near nodding, but he thinks that I would get in the car with him. I looked at Cina rolling my eyes. I grabbed Tasia hand and she started to whine about walking. I looked at her, letting her know that I wasn't having her shit today, and she got her attitude together long enough for us to walk home.

"Nigga, she doesn't want you. Leave her the fuck alone, shit. Y'all all getting on my fucking nerves!" Cina screamed as Tasia and I made it to the front door.

I could hear Rita talking shit through the phone. When I heard a door slam, I already knew that Cina was slamming doors, which means her and Rita are about to really go at it. I know that Rita doesn't want her over there. Cina told me that the only reason why she filled a report saying that she had runaway was because Cina's auntie stopped bringing her money. She figured that she could start back getting that and more with Cina being back in the house.

"Who you talking to?" I heard somebody say in the background.

"Meria, she's leaving for school tomorrow," Cina replied.

"Bitch, who is you talking to? Why are you telling all my business?" I asked as Tasia and I made it to the house.

"Shut up, bitch, it's just Scar. He been coming by, checking on me and the baby."

"I got to go. Call me if you need something," Scar said, sounding like he was in a hurry.

"Where he going? To see that hoe Felicia?" I asked, laughing.

"Bitch, he can hear you. You on speaker," Cina said.

"Yo' mouth. Nigga, if you were nigga, I'd beat yo—" Scar attempted to say before I cut him right the fuck off.

"You wouldn't do shit if I was a nigga. R'Shad, I'm not scared of you. I know that everybody thinks you so crazy and always be kissing yo' ass but nigga, I'm not the one!" I spat, meaning every word.

"You ain't seen crazy. You used to fuckin' with weird ass niggas. The fucked-up thing is you don't even know what a real solid ass nigga looks like because every nigga that done had you was a fucking bum or a worker. Get you a nigga that could even come close to be being me and then we can discuss the type of nigga I am, sweetheart," Scar spat into the phone.

"Fuck you!" I said all delayed because he definitely tried to read me.

Cina started laughing and let me know that Scar was off the porch and couldn't hear me. I can't stand him. Looking out of my bedroom window, I saw Scar pulling up to Pumpkin's house. I could hear Rita talking shit and giving Cina a list of shit to tell Scar that she needs for the baby. I pray that Cina's circumstances hurry up and change because she shouldn't have to go through all this living with Rita and she's pregnant.

"R'Shad!" I screamed out the window.

He started looking around, trying to see who was

calling him as he got out of the car he was driving. Every other day, this nigga is in a different car. He done came a long way and it ain't hard to tell that he just has taken over in Chaos's absence. R'Shad finally realized where I was at and flicked me off.

"I would never fuck you!"

"That's why you screaming across the street on my dick, damn near stalking me. Sameria, what did I eat for breakfast this morning? Don't get to Texas and fall in love with another broke ass nigga," R'Shad said while laughing.

18

SCAR

"Pumpkin, you need to go over there to check on Cina and make sure that she's good," I said, plopping down on the couch.

"I don't need to do shit for that bitch. Her and her momma are the reason why my baby is locked up now. Fuck that bitch! You keep taking yo' ass over there to check on her and letting her and her momma use yo' ass up. So clearly, I know that the bitch is alive," Pumpkin said and proceeded to take pulls from her cigarette.

"You know how she feel about that nigga Ricardo and you. That shit's all her momma and the state on this bullshit. Pumpkin, you need to chill. How the fuck you gon' explain this shit to Ricardo when he comes home? He not gon' want to hear that shit that you weren't there for her. You already know how he's going to feel about that. I barely know the bitch but on the strength of my brother and because I know he'd do the same, I'm going to make sure she's good," I said, trying to get Pumpkin to quit being so fucking petty and shit. I got all this other shit I need to be taking care of.

Cina is getting big as hell and every time I go and check on her, she just sitting in the house looking sad as hell like she been crying all day. Luckily, Yoni, on the strength of Ricardo, still fucking with her, so she can do her thing with the nails and shit. When she does call, she asks about Pumpkin just as much as she asks about Ricardo. Her and Pumpkin were close as hell until this bullshit went down. Pumpkin went hard for Cina and treated her like she was one of us.

"Nigga, I ain't you. I don't have shit to say to her," Pumpkin nagged for the hundredth time.

Knock, Knock, knock.

"Nigga, what you waiting for? Get the damn door," Pumpkin demanded.

"Why can't you get the door?" I asked, looking over at Pumpkin.

"Nigga, because I'm not. It's not nobody for me. I don't have no damn friends coming to see me," Pumpkin spat, not even budging to get the door.

"That's yo' problem. You need to get some damn friends, so you can stay out of my business," I said as I got up to get the door.

Since Ricardo been gone, everything been falling on me. Antonio did step up and get his shit together. I was hesitant to fuck with him at all because of the bullshit that he was doing. Then the day that Ricardo got arrested, I got a phone call that Antonio was beating Tay up at the fucking gas station. I don't give a fuck about that dumb bitch, but he caused issues for us in the streets with her cousins. Shit been quiet and that's one of the only reasons that I still been fucking with him.

"Naw, this ain't a good idea, not right now," I said, trying to close the door because I don't have time for this shit today.

"R'Shad, no, please. I just want to talk to Pumpkin. I need to talk to her," Cina begged, putting her swollen foot in the door, blocking me from closing it.

It's been damn near two months that Pumpkin been tripping with her. I don't have shit else to say, I'm going to let them figure this shit out on they own. I stepped back, so Cina could come in, and I noticed that the whole left side of her face was bruised. Her hair is all over her head, her makeup ain't done and she didn't look like herself. Cina's the type of bitch that always keeps herself together. I never seen her with her hair and nails not done. She got nails missing and shit like she been fighting.

"What the fuck is going on? You good?" I asked, already knowing the fucking answer.

"Naw, but I'll be alright," Cina replied and sighed hard.

Cina made her way in the house and I could hear her trying to explain everything that done went down to Pumpkin, but Pumpkin ain't saying shit back. My phone started ringing and I know that it's Fe. Fe started going to school about a month ago, so we ain't spent that much time together. Fe and I moved together, but she been talking shit about how I'm hardly ever there. Shit, I always make time for her, but she needs to understand that it's shit that I have to take care of and make sure shit is all the way right.

Pumpkin doesn't fuck with Fe at all, so I damn near

be having to drag her over here. I come over here every day because I have to make sure my auntie is good. Pumpkin talks shit and she is petty as hell, but she was down with a nigga in a way that I can never pay her back. Now it's like she is going through it all over again with my brother. She been stressed out and even though she won't admit it, I know her, and I can tell that she is going through it.

"What's up?" I said as I sat down in a chair on the porch, answering Fe's call.

"When are you coming home?" Fe whined into the phone.

"I'll be there," I said as I heard something that caught my attention.

I tried to get Felicia off the phone, but she wasn't trying to hear anything that I had to say. I put her on mute and made my way in the house. She doesn't need to know shit that's going on with my family, so she can tell her messy ass family. Cina was still in here begging for Pumpkin to forgive her and trying to plead her case that she didn't want any of this to happen. Pumpkin is a fucking asshole and even though she knows that Cina isn't lying, she still feels betrayed because of how hard she rides for her family.

"What do you mean yo' momma wanted you to set my brother up?" I spat as I walked into the house.

"She's been trying to get me to set him up... Now, y'all up. I was... shit, I was scared to tell Ricardo because I didn't know how he was going to react. Pumpkin, you know me, and you know that I would never do nothing like that to him. I love him, and y'all know that," Cina whined and tears started rapidly falling from her already swollen eyes.

"Don't talk that *I know you* shit. If this was something that yo' raggedy ass momma been plotting on my baby, then yo' ass should have said something. Not laying up in my house, letting Ricardo take care of you and then they trying to make it seem like he been holding you hostage. Bitch, they are trying their best to put that shit on me all because you were scared. Bitch, be scared about being a single parent!" Pumpkin spat and stormed out the room, bumping into me on her way out.

"Sit, right here. Don't move!" I spat and made my way to talk to Pumpkin as the house phone started ringing.

"Tell, him. Tell him what you doing to Brittney," I said, hovering over Pumpkin in the kitchen.

"Nigga, get from over me. You not my damn daddy!" Pumpkin spat and attempted to push me, but I didn't budge.

When we're talking about Cina, we say Brittney because the calls are being recorded and the last thing my brother needs is to risk catching another charge? Me and Pumpkin have been going to see him once a week, and we talk to him every day. From day one to the day he comes home, we have his back though it all. Pumpkin beating around the bush and ain't said shit that she needs to say to Ricardo. Stressing him out more ain't what he needs, but Pumpkin needs to quit lying too.

"Tell him the truth, P. Tell em' what the fuck you doing to his bitch," I said, still standing over her.

"Shut the fuck up, R'Shad. I'll go and talk to the bitch. Let me talk to my baby," Pumpkin said covering the phone, so Ricardo couldn't hear her.

I kissed Pumpkin on the cheek, and she tried pushing me off her. Once I was sure that she knows I'm done dealing with this bullshit with her and Cina, I made my way back to Cina, so that we could have a clear understanding about some shit. I know how Ricardo feels about Cina and the way that she carries herself, I don't see her being a grimy bitch and being on some bullshit, but I don't put shit past nobody. As I made my way back in the living room, Cina was on her phone doing something. I can tell that she got a lot of shit on her mind, but she ain't said shit. I don't have no time to waste, so playing fucking games like she be doing with my brother, that shit ain't gon' work with me.

"Look, I need to know exactly what the fuck yo' momma on? Don't leave out shit. I need to know everything you know. Who the fuck else has yo' momma been talking to about this shit?" I said back to back, not stopping for air while sitting down in the chair across from her.

"Scar, I'll tell you everything, but—" Cina attempted to say before I lost my patience and cut her off.

"Ain't no fucking buts with this shit! I'm trying to be cool because I can see you already going thru enough shit right now. What the fuck I won't do for you or no other bitch is not make sure my brother is protected. I need to know right fucking now whose side are you on?" I spat, trying to stay calm, but now hovering over Cina. New tears started to fall down her face to place the ones that had dried up.

～

"WHO ARE YOU?" A bitch asked through the intercom.

"Scar!" I spat, losing my patience.

After finding out that bullshit yesterday about Cina and her momma, I hit the streets. The only way to clear my mind and think is for me to get some money. I ain't been to sleep yet, but I made a bag last night. This nigga, Sevino, just had one of his people meet me and give me the address, so he knows I'm coming. This nigga is acting like a bitch, I got other shit to do. This nigga got less than a minute to open this fucking door or I'm out. My phone started ringing. Pulling it out, I see it was Fe. I'm on my way to the house when I leave here, so I didn't answer. Turning to leave, I pulled out my phone to check out some other options.

"Damn, nigga! You need to get some fucking patience," Sevino suggested from behind me.

"Time waits for nobody, and I don't have no time to waste," I replied, turning around.

"My bad, I was handling some shit that just came up," Sevino said, stepping back so I could come in the house.

I didn't waste my time saying anything because why he had me waiting doesn't matter. My brother was supposed to be here, but with his current situation, that shit ain't possible. Sevino led the way through his house. He lives all the way the fuck out in the middle of nowhere. We made our way through the house, down a long ass hallway and went into a room that must be his office.

"Where's Chaos?" Sevino asked as he sat down behind his desk and lit a blunt.

"He got locked up," I said, not wanting to say too much as he tried to pass me the blunt.

"I'm good," I said, leaning back and checking out the room.

Looking around the room, I saw pictures of him, his family and his niggas. Other than my brother, Antonio and my best friend, Zone, I don't fuck with no other niggas. Fucking with Sevino can put us in a better position. Right now, my focus is getting shit right so I can always be good.

"I like the way you move, and I know that we can make a lot of money together," Sevino said, putting his blunt in the ashtray.

"You already done said that more than once. I know what the fuck I can move, and I know what the fuck I can bring to the table," I spat, not impressed by none of the shit that I done already heard.

Sevino sent a message to me through Meezy because I had been putting him off until I knew what was going to happen with Ricardo. After talking to Zone, I decided that I could come and chop it up with him to see what he had to say. I know that Sevino needs us him and his cousin Teflon done made a big come up here lately. Listening to him talk, he still ain't said shit to me that makes me want to do business with him.

As Sevino laid out what we can do, I started to think that fucking with him ain't gon' benefit us just make him more money. Yea, this nigga got some cars, jewelry and shit, but this nigga still fucks with rat bitches from the hood, so he ain't what the fuck he thinks he is. If I was easily impressed then I would just jump for the opportunity to eat with this nigga, but I'll never let a nigga downplay who the fuck I am and how me and my niggas are getting it.

"That ain't gon' work. I don't know who the fuck you thought you were talking to, but you not about to low ball me," I spat, standing up to leave.

"Nigga, I'm definitely not trying to play y'all. I see what y'all doing and the work that Ricardo put in with that nigga Cash. I already know that y'all hungry and what we can do together, but damn, nigga. I'm trying to bring you to my table," Sevino said, sitting back in his chair and picking back up his blunt.

I could see from the look on his face that he wasn't expecting me to say what I said. We held out for as long as we did, so that he would come back with a better deal. He's offering what Ricardo and I discussed would be the best deal, but I'm still not satisfied. I know the way that I hustle and get shit done.

"What is it that y'all asking for?" Sevino finally said.

"We need 70/30 and we'll—" I attempted to say as Sevino cut me off.

"Nigga, seventy? Are you crazy?" Sevino said, leaning forward in his chair onto his desk, putting his blunt out and staring into my eyes.

"You know what I'm on and how I get down. And we'll buy double what we originally discussed." Standing up to leave, I knew that he had some shit that he needs to think about, so I saw my way out the house.

He'll be in touch after word gets back to him with the shit that I did last night. As I made my way to the front of the house, I could hear a bitch screaming at the top of her lungs and glass breaking. That shit ain't none of my business, so I made my way outside. My phone started ringing and it was the call that I'd been waiting for. As I pulled away from Sevino's, I saw the same bitch that was sitting in the living room when I walked in, throwing shit into his circular driveway. Seeing that shit just makes me think about the shit Fe been on.

After I got the information that I needed from the person on my line, I ended the call and made my way home. Fe been going to school and shit, and I'm all for that shit because that's what she wants to do. When she ain't in school, she's always with her thot ass sisters. I don't give a fuck about her hanging out every once in a while and shit, but damn, you ain't gotta be in the club every weekend. She doesn't understand that shit. Where I'm trying to go to with this hustlin' shit, I cannot have my bitch out here like that.

Pulling up to the house, I saw Fe's car in the driveway and her sister's car parked in front of the house. Zai is cool, and she fucks with my nigga Zone, but she stays on some hoe shit. Pulling into the driveway, my phone started ringing. It was Ricardo. I'm not telling him what happened with Sevino because I know that he's going to come back with what I want real soon.

"You coming to court tomorrow?" Ricardo asked as the call connected.

"I already told you I'm going to be there," I spat as I walked into the house through the garage.

Zai, Felicia and Tay were so damn loud, I could barely hear what Ricardo was saying. "Y'all can pipe the fuck down or take y'all fucking conversation outside. I can't even hear my fucking brother," I spat, making my way through the living room. Fe jumped up and followed behind me.

"We better shut up because you know that nigga

crazy, and he will kick us out," Tay said as I made my way upstairs.

"Yea, bitch, so you might want to shut fuck up before yo' ass is outside like Denver Housing Authority did all yo' momma's shit!" I yelled down the stairs.

"Baby, chill. Who you on the phone with?" Fe asked.

"My brother. Kick them hoes out and get dressed," I replied and slapped Fe on the ass as she left our room to kick them bitches out.

"Did you handle that?" Ricardo asked, referring to the situation with Sevino.

"Yea, I'm handling it."

Ricardo didn't respond, he just blew hard into the phone. All of our life, he always wanted to be the one in charge and making all the decisions. Him being in his current position, making decisions isn't something he can do. With him being locked up, someone is making every decision for him, and I know that is killing him. I finished talking to my brother until he had to get off the phone, telling him about how shit is going with Cina.

"Where are we going?" Fe asked as I went through the closet looking for something to wear.

"Just get dressed," I said as I noticed a bag full of ink tags that were taken off some clothes.

"What's this?" I asked and by the look on Fe's face, she knows that I'm mad as hell.

"Shit, Zai must have left them here," Fe said, trying to snatch the grocery store bag out of my hand that was filled with ink tags and security tags.

"So, Zai hit a lick, came here to take the tags off and some way the bag ended up in this closet? Don't play with me, Fe!" I spat, threw the bag of tags in Felicia's face and made my way out the closet.

"Wait R'Shad! Listen!"

"I'm not listening to shit! We've already had this conversation, so you knew what the fuck it was. Then you gon' sit in my face and lie like I'm some fucking goofy! You just can't leave this shit alone. What the fuck is you going to school for? You want to be out every night, shakin' yo' ass, gettin' drunk and come to find out, you still doing this bullshit! For what? Tell me that. Whatever you want, nigga, I make sure that you get it!" I screamed. I know she felt every word that I said because she jumped like I was 'bout to fucking hit her.

"You won't even give me a chance to talk, damn. You're never here! Yea, you buy me some shit and you pay the bills, but all you care about is Pumpkin and yo' brother!" Fe whined.

"What the fuck do you want me to do, sit in the house with you all day ? You know what the fuck I'm doing! I'm not about to keep explaining that to you. I know you 'bout to bring up some shit that Zone did yesterday, and I don't want to hear that shit either! I can't make Pumpkin like you. She's a fucking asshole and some days, she don't even fuck with me!" I spat and turned to walk away.

"You just had to do shit yo' way instead of even thinking about the shit that I had on the table for you for when you came home," Felicia admitted what her fucking issue was finally.

"We've had this conversation. I don't fuck with none of yo' people like that, and I'm not doing business with them. I don't give a fuck how much money they got and what type of cars they drivin'. What part don't yo' ass get?

I'm rocking with my brother and if that's a fucking problem for you, then yo' ass can go!"

I already told her what it was and we not hurtin'. We doin' better than them niggas and she think they doin' somethin'. I know that people rock with their family because that's what you supposed to do, but my bitch is supposed to rock with me over anybody. This is becoming a fucking headache, and I don't know how much more I can take.

I made my way downstairs because this shit ain't gon' work. Shit, we sat down and talked about everything and she's the one who said that she was done. How the fuck that look, my bitch out stealing and shit? We could have stayed in the hood if she still wanted to be on that shit. My phone started ringing and looking at it, I saw that it's Zone.

"Damn nigga! Why did you have to put Zai out? I had shit to do, and she just popped up on a nigga," Zone said as soon as the phone connected.

"Nigga, her sister 'bout to be with her in a minute, so you ain't gon' have to worry about the bitch," I spat, looking through the mail that's on the counter.

"You just gon' get on the phone when we in the middle of fuckin' talkin'?" Fe said with an attitude like she got a reason to be mad, like I did some fuck shit to her.

"I need you to follow me to drop off this car and shoot me somewhere real quick."

"Say less, I'm 'bout to pull up. My nigga always comes through with a reason to get rid of this bitch," Zone replied, meaning every word.

I laughed and looked up. Fe was still standing in front

of me with an attitude, but she ain't said shit. This arguing shit is getting old, just when I think that shit is changing for the better, but I'm not about to keep dealing with this shit. More than anything, the lying shit ain't something that I'm putting up with from nobody, not even her ass.

"I was there for you when everybody told me that I should leave you alone," Fe whined.

"Bitch, I wasn't holding you hostage. Don't try to throw up in my face some shit that you did for me to try to make it seem like I'm in the wrong because I don't want some rat bitch that's running from mall security and yo' picture up at the hair store for stealing weave," I spa,t folding up the two bills that I needed to pay and stuffing them in my back pocket.

"You not gon' talk to me like I'm some bum bitch. Let's talk about how the fuck you think it's okay for you to come in this house after the sun comes up! Where the fuck were you at last night?" Fe asked, raising her voice too loud for me.

"Lower yo' fucking voice when you talkin' to me. You know where I was at because I talked to yo' ass several times. I'm gon' give you some time to get yo' mind right and figure out what the fuck you want. If you want to keep doin' bullshit, then do that, but yo ass won't be doing that shit with me. I moved us out here. You could have stayed yo' ass in the fuckin' hood if that's what the fuck you wanted to be on," I spat as Zone texted me, letting me know he was outside.

"So, you think that it's okay for you just to leave instead of staying to work this out? Fuck it, then leave. Do you know how many niggas would love to fuck with me?

It's plenty of niggas that I been swerving to stay loyal to yo' stupid ass," Fe said, folding her arms across her chest, leaning back against the counter and mugging me.

"You know me. So, don't play with me, Felicia. You and any nigga that you think about fixing yo' mouth to speak to will come up missing!" I barked then left her stupid ass sitting there looking dumb as I made my way out the house.

As I made my way to the car, I saw Felicia standing in the doorway just looking. I know she wants to say some bullshit, but she ain't crazy. Causing a scene and embarrassing me ain't some shit that I'm going to tolerate. Fe made her way back in the house, slamming the door so hard that all the windows in the front of the house started shaking.

"What the fuck is wrong with her? She ain't got shit to complain about, all the shit that you do for her. You do too damn much. That's making Zai think that I'm supposed to do the same shit for her," Zone complained.

"That's my bitch, I'm supposed to do for her. But you fuckin' Zai and several other hoes. You gon' go broke doing for all them bitches," I replied.

"Damn, nigga! Tell every damn body all my damn business. You know Felicia nosy and probably heard yo' ass. Now I'm gon' have to hear Zai's fucking mouth about that."

Shrugging my shoulders, I got into the car and rolled down my window. "If you put yo' bitches in they place, you wouldn't have so many problems," I said and skirted off, so I could turn in this car. I got a call that my car is ready to be picked up. Ricardo wanted me to get Cina a car so she can get around and handle all her business and shit, but after the shit she told me about her momma and cousin, all that's on pause. Ricardo will understand why when she's able to tell him the truth.

I dropped off the rental, and we made it over to the dealership in about forty-five minutes. When I got there, shit wasn't right or ready, but I gave my mans, Bobby, that Zone introduced me to some more money to speed up the process and get it right. We made it out the dealership in about thirty minutes which was just what the fuck I needed because I don't have all night. Since Fe is on some other shit, I made my way over to Pumpkin's so I could wait for my meeting at midnight. When I got to Pumpkin's, she wasn't there, which surprised me because she doesn't really go nowhere. I figured she just ran out to the store and she'd be back soon. Flopping down on the couch, I turned on the TV, ignoring my ringing phone. I don't have shit to say to Felicia. I'm starting to question everything about her ass, and if I got to question my bitch, I don't need her.

"What that bitch do?" Pumpkin asked, shaking her head as she walked in the house.

"Some bullshit," I said, turning up the TV.

"I know you heard that nigga knocking on the door! Just standing in front of my damn house!" Pumpkin screamed from the kitchen.

I jumped up because clearly just cutting him off wasn't enough. He still doesn't get the picture, I don't got shit for him. Zion started off solid, but that bitch broke that nigga. He started fucking up bad, being late, coming up short and shit. I was starting to think he was smoking that shit.

"Look, nigga, you been acting like a bitch ever since

Sameria left! I don't have time to babysit no nigga!" I yelled, wasting no time once I got outside.

"Nigga, I know that I fucked up and shit went left. I was dealing with some shit. I'm back right now and ready to get shit back on track. I got a lil shorty that I got to make sure is good," Zion replied.

"Nigga, I can't do shit for you," I said and made my way back in the house.

"You don't always got to be so fucking evil. You could have given that boy another chance. Shit, you gave Antonio more than one chance, and he ain't gon' ever be shit," Pumpkin wasted no time saying as I walked back in the house.

"That was because of you and Ricardo. I'm not doing that shit for everybody then everybody will think that that's how this works."

"Have you talked to Antonio?" Pumpkin asked.

"Earlier, but I'll see him in a sec. Why?"

Pumpkin didn't answer me, she got up and left the living room. By her response, I already know it's some bullshit. She knows how I'm going to react, so it's best that she doesn't tell me and she already knows that. That's her son, and I swear she talks more shit about him than anybody else. Pumpkin always says that she knew he wasn't right for a long time, but he's still her baby.

"Damn, I'm hungry too," I said as Pumpkin came back in the room with a big ass plate.

"Go to yo' house and eat. You need to watch Antonio."

"What you waitin' for? Tell me what that hoe did," Pumpkin asked, referring to Fe.

"Give me some, and I'll tell you," I said, trying to get to Pumpkin's plate.

"You get on my damn nerves. Huh, R'Shad, shit," Pumpkin complained, handing me her plate.

I started telling Pumpkin about the shit that's been going on with me and Felicia. I know how Pumpkin feels about Fe, but I tell her everything. Through everything, right or wrong, Pumpkin gon' ride with me. I just need some space because it's some shit that ain't gon' work with me for any bitch. The way shit is changing, I want to take Fe with me, but I ain't taking a rat bitch to have me out here looking like a goof.

"You know who I want you to be with," Pumpkin said like I'm supposed to know who the fuck she talkin' about.

"Who, Pumpkin?"

"Sameria. She's pretty, smart and she gon' do something with her life. You trying to make Fe into what Sameria already is. That bitch is dumb and she ain't gon' ever be more than what she is. That girl been fucked off her whole life and nothin' is going to change that. Don't have no baby with that slow bitch."

"My bitch ain't slow. You always talking about that bitch Sameria, she ain't nothing special."

"Nigga, what do you know? You fuckin' with a bitch that's in the streets as much as you. She out there fuckin'," Pumpkin assured me.

"She definitely ain't doing that," I said for a fact, making my way to the kitchen.

Pumpkin quick to jump to that whenever we talk about Felicia. Ricardo needs to hurry up and get out so Pumpkin can have somebody else business to be in. She hates Tay more than she does Felicia. She done beat Tay's ass several times, so she doesn't want anything to do with her or she would be in her and Antonio business.

"Come on, we need to get to the hospital! Cina just called!" Pumpkin frantically yelled from the living room.

"The hospital for what? She not due yet," I said, checking the time.

"Nigga, quit asking me fuckin' questions and come the fuck on!" Pumpkin demanded as I snatched up my keys off the table and followed her out the front door.

Shit, I thought we had some more time before she had the baby. I wanted this fucking case behind us, so that my brother could be there. Shit, I ain't trying to deal with this shit. I jumped in the car and pulled off, so we could go check on Cina. Pumpkin was on the phone with Tricky loud as hell and my phone started going off. It was a Texas number. I don't know nobody in Texas, so I ignored it.

"Nigga, what you so damn nervous for? Nigga, you supposed to be a thug! What the fuck, you scared about a baby being born?" Pumpkin taunted, trying to hit me.

"I'm not a fucking nervous, it ain't my baby. I just want my fuckin brother to be home, so he can deal with this shit."

"He's coming home and everything, is going to be okay," Pumpkin reassured me, but I'm not so sure.

I don't have no fucking faith in the system. Them people do whatever the fuck they want to do. Even with the lawyer, I ain't so sure because of the bullshit that I know Cina's momma will do. With all the bullshit that Cina told us that her momma did and what she is planning, I still don't trust her all the way. When I told Ricardo what the deal was when me and Pumpkin went to see him, I know that shit put him in a fucked-up position. I know that Ricardo felt a fucking way when I told him how I felt about his bitch, but I don't give a fuck because at the end of the day I got to make sure we good.

We made it to the hospital, and Pumpkin jumped out the fucking car before I could put it in park. My phone started ringing and it was that Texas number again. I answered as I made my way into the hospital. Pumpkin didn't even wait for a nigga, she ran into the hospital.

"Who this?" I spat.

"Is Cina okay?" A female asked into the phone.

"Who the fuck is this?"

"Sameria, R'Shad! Cina not answering the phone! I been calling her for hours!" Sameria whined.

"How the fuck did you get my number?" I asked as I scanned the emergency room looking for Pumpkin.

"Does it matter, R'Shad? Have you talked to Cee? I'm worried about her, she always answers."

"I ain't Cina's muthafuckin' secretary. Maybe she doesn't want to talk to yo' ass no mo', I wouldn't."

Click.

I hung up on Sameria's ass and listened to Pumpkin cuss out this bitch at the desk. This is not what the fuck I had in mind for tonight. Why the fuck would this bitch call Pumpkin if we can't even see her. I don't have time for this shit. I already know that Rita's ass got something to do with us not being allowed to see her.

"Bitch, just do yo' fucking job and get to callin'!" Pumpkin screamed, catching everybody in the waiting room's attention.

"Ma'am, what you need to do is calm down. Talking to me that way—" The woman attempted to say before Pumpkin tried to jump over the desk on her ass and I grabbed her, but she was able to grab the lady's fuckin' hair.

"P, chill. Mannn, you need to chill out before they kick us the fuck out of here," I lectured, prying her hand out this bitch's dry ass hair.

"I'm calling the police!" The woman screamed bloody murder like something was really wrong with her ass.

"Bitch, shut up. All she did was pull yo' fucking hair, hoe!" I spat, losing my patience and reaching in my pocket.

Throwing a few bills for her fucked-up ass weave at the bitch and then I got Pumpkin to calm down. This other bitch came over to help us with the security guard standing by her like we were going to do something to her. It's about to be a long fucking night. This bitch ass security guard is getting on my fucking nerves.

"Are you the dad? If it's a boy, he's going to look just like you. Are you and the mom together?" The bitch supposed to be helping us asked, playing with her tongue on the last question.

"What's yo' name?" I spat and looked back at Pumpkin who was on the phone talking shit loud enough for everybody in here to hear her, sitting down behind me.

"Mercedes."

"Look, bitch, I don't want you. Mercedes, bitch you don't even have no fuckin' edges. Just do yo' muthafuckin' job. Can we see Cina Miller or not?"

19

CINA

I been at the hospital for hours as they ran test after test to make sure that I'm good. My mom was in and out the room, getting on my nerves. I just wish that she would leave because she damn sure ain't helping me. My whole pregnancy she has made each day worse than the last, since I been back at her house. I called Pumpkin and let her know I was at the hospital because I'm spotting. They are worried about the baby and my arms keep going numb.

Not having nobody by my side while I'm going through this by myself, I wouldn't wish on anybody. I haven't heard from Unique in days and when I do hear from her ass, all she wants to know is what she can get from me. She always needs to borrow a few dollars 'til Friday, but when Friday comes, that bitch goes missing. I don't give a fuck about the money, it just would be nice to have somebody be here with me while I'm going through this.

"Can I see my phone?" I asked. I knew that my

momma felt my attitude as she rushed over to the hospital bed and smacked me so hard, I started to see stars.

"Bitch, don't get no muthafuckin' attitude with me, you won't ever get this phone back. Keep fuckin' wit' me," my momma said through gritted teeth.

Knock, Knock, Knock.

"Come in," my momma said.

Two of the doctors that have been coming in and out and a woman that I haven't seen followed in behind them and a nurse. Somebody knocking on the door is the only thing that stopped Rita from keep going with her bullshit. The thought of anybody finding out who she really is would only slow up the money that she is planning on being able to get. She was holding my phone tight because hers is cut off. I give her money that should at least last her a couple days and then she has her hand out asking for more. I'm hiding my money at Pumpkin's and the bank, so that I can have something, because leaving anything at her house is hers in her head.

"Ms. Miller, we need you to fill out some papers. If you can go with Mercedes here, she can show you where you need to go," Doctor Aurora said.

"Have y'all figured out what is going on with my baby?" My mom asked, getting closer to me and caressing me like she gives a fuck.

"We're still working on it," Dr. Aurora replied.

My momma made her way out the room with Mercedes and Doctor Aurora stood directly in front of the door. Dr. Smith made her way over to my bedside and the way that she is looking at me is making me uncomfortable. Doctor Aurora is trying to give the impression that everything is okay, but I can tell that something is wrong. Why the fuck didn't she want to say whatever it is in front of my momma?

"Is it something wrong with my baby?" I asked, looking back and forth between both of them, rubbing my stomach, trying to see if my baby will move.

"No, No. She is fine," Dr. Aurora pleaded.

"Where did the marks come from on your arms?" Dr. Smith questioned, staring a hole through me.

"I bumped into something," I replied, shrugging my shoulders.

"I know that this can be a scary situation, but we want to help you. We need you to trust us and tell us the truth. We are mandatory reporters. Do you know what that means?" Dr. Aurora asked coming over to my side.

"No," I answered, leaning back on the bed, trying to get comfortable.

"We are obligated by law to report any known or suspected child abuse," Dr. Aurora pleaded.

"I'm not being fuckin' abused," I lied.

"Cina, we see the bruises and it was reported how your mother has been talking to you. I know that this is a difficult situation, but I'm going to be honest with you. Right now, you need to worry about not only the safety of you, but your unborn child. We are willing to do every- thing that we can to help, but we need you to be honest with us. This is Taniece, she is a social worker. Would you like us to stay in the room while you talk to her? We really want to help you, Cina," Dr. Smith assured me.

I didn't say anything. My mind started to run a mile a minute because me lying and telling them bullshit is one thing. The thing is, them completing investigations and shit like I know they will is something totally different. Suffering through hell with my mom ain't that hard because I know what to expect from her and I know that I'm not going to have to deal with it forever. Soon, Ricardo will be home, and I'll be the fuck out of her house.

"Cina, we need to know a few things, so that we can do whatever needs to be done so that we can help you and your baby girl." Taniece said as she came closer to me.

Looking up at her, I realized that she is the same social worker that picked me up from Yoni's shop. This bitch made me go back with my momma, but she wants me to believe that she can help me. I didn't recognize her at first, and I know my momma didn't because she wouldn't have left the room so easily. Taniece done lost a lot of weight, cut and dyed her hair. The thought of ending up in the system isn't something that I want for me and damn sure not my baby.

"I told y'all I'm not being abused. Just leave me the fuck alone," I spat, looking up at the ceiling.

"To make this easier for you, we need you to talk to us," Dr. Aurora pleaded again.

"I need to talk to Pumpkin. Can y'all go to the lobby and see if she's down there?" I replied, still looking at the ceiling as tears burned my eyes. I held them back, refusing to let them fall.

"I'll go and see if I can find her," Dr. Aurora responded and made her way out the room.

"I know this isn't easy. I know that you have a lot going on right now. I know what you are dealing with a lot of different emotions and on top of that, your body is changing," Taniece pleaded and attempted to sit at the end of the hospital bed.

"You know what I'm going through? No, the fuck you don't! I told you that she was lying, and Ricardo was not putting his hands on me, but what did you do about that? Nothing, and he's still in jail! Just get Pumpkin!" I roared. She backed all the way up and hurried over by Dr. Smith.

Dr. Smith and Taniece both made their way out the room. I turned down the TV, trying to hear what they were saying, but I couldn't. As bad as I want to, my big ass can't run out of here. I can barely walk down that long ass hall without being out of breath. I damn sure ain't going to be able to run out of here without anybody catching me. I just want to talk to Pumpkin before I do anything.

When I showed up at her house that day, I didn't know how she was going to react. Pumpkin was pissed, and I had been calling for what felt like forever, but that was a little over a month and she wasn't trying to hear shit I had to say. I'd be lying if I said that Scar didn't scare the fuck out of me because he did. Everybody says that his ass is crazy and that he killed his dad. The way that nigga was looking at me that night, I thought I was going to be next. I know how Scar feels about Ricardo. That nigga will fuck some shit up when it comes to his brother, and Ricardo feels the same way. Nobody can't even mention Scar's name in a bad way without Ricardo going the fuck off, and it usually takes a lot for him to even trip.

"Are you okay?" Pumpkin asked as she barged in the room without even knocking.

"Yea, I'm alright. I need to talk to you," I replied, looking to see if I saw anybody by the door because she damn sure didn't close it behind her.

"Bitch, get to talking. That lady said we got five minutes. They are down the hall," Pumpkin said, doubling back to close the door and throwing her purse in the chair on the side of my bed.

I told Pumpkin everything that I needed to tell her. She took it all in and surprisingly hasn't said anything, which was making me worry. Even though she let me back in her life, this lady is crazy and liable to kick me right back out without blinking twice. She's stubborn as hell, but the weight that Ricardo has with her is the only reason why she still deals with me, and I already know that. I wish that I could just go home with her, but I know that isn't an option, not until the charges against Ricardo go away.

"You're going to be okay. We got you. As much as you and fucking Ricardo get on my damn nerves, you're family. And no matter what, Cina, I will do everything I can to make sure that you and the baby are okay while Ricardo is gone" Pumpkin said as she plopped down beside me.

"I don't know where they are going to send me. What if I can't talk to y'all?" I pleaded, still not sure about what I needed to do.

"Cina, there is no way no way that I can sneak yo' big ass out this hospital. I don't kidnap bitches. We'll figure it out. I know damn well we ain't supposed to be talking to each other now. These fuckin' people are dumb as hell," Pumpkin assured me and slipped me a phone as someone knocked on the door.

Looking at the phone, I saw that it was Ricardo's phone and I put it in bra. Dr. Smith and Dr. Aurora made their way in the room with Taniece following behind. As they came in the room, nobody said anything. That made me fucking mad because I could already tell it's about to be some bullshit. Just when I think that things are going to get better, boom, some more bullshit happens. Every day it's something else.

"Am I going to be able to communicate with her?" Pumpkin blurted out, breaking the silence.

"We'll see what we can do," Taniece replied, biting her bottom lip.

"So, basically that means no. Let's get this shit over with," I spat getting out the bed and putting my clothes on.

"Well, can you at least explain to me what is going on? Where are you taking her?" Pumpkin asked.

Taniece started to explain to her what was happening and that she was searching for an emergency placement for me. I've never been in trouble and shit, at least halfway did everything that I was supposed to do, but none of that matters. Both of these fucking doctors kept saying that they wanted to help and all this bullshit, but while I'm going through this shit, neither one of them are going to be able to help. As much as I hate Rita, I damn sure would have rather gone home with her than wherever the fuck I'm going.

Pumpkin walked over to where I was leaning against the widow seal waiting for Taniece to tell me any damn thing at this point. She hugged me tight and that caught me off guard. My daughter started moving all crazy, so shit, I know she was surprised too. Pumpkin damn sure has never hugged me.

"Call me or text me if you can't call. Everything is going to be good. I'll let you know what happens at court tomorrow," Pumpkin whispered and let me go. With each step that Pumpkin took to make her way out the room, I felt more and more alone. I just want to go to sleep, so I can wake up and shit is different. This can't be life.

"You're going to be fine. I am not going to go home until I make sure that you are in a safe place," Taniece predicted, but I'll believe it when I see it.

It's hard for me to believe that. Who knows where the fuck I'm going to end up tonight? The doctors cleared me to go and let me know that I needed to get some rest. They assured me that I'll be fine after they got the results back for the last test. They explained to me that the spotting that I was seeing was from a polyp that was due to the increase in estrogen. I was relieved, but now I have more shit that is going to stress me out even more than I've already been. Dealing with my pregnancy damn near by myself is already hard. I mean, Pumpkin and R'Shad are here for me whenever I call them, but they could never take the place of Ricardo being there. I should be planning my baby shower and getting everything together for my daughter, but that's not my reality.

"Come on. Let's go and get something to eat," Taniece said, trying to wrap her arm around me.

"Don't fucking touch me!" I spat, snatching away.

I stormed into the bathroom, so that I could text Meria and tell her what's going on. I don't want to take the chance of Taniece catching me on the phone and having to give it up, so I sat in the stall and called her. That bitch Taniece can wait. She claims she ain't going home until she finds somewhere safe for me to go, so she can start looking now.

20

SAMERIA

I love being down here, even though it's hot as hell. I'd be lying if I said that I wasn't missing home. I've been home-sick as hell and not being able to talk to Cina like I want to has been really bothering me. It's been a month since she's been in the group home. She hates it and I hate it just as much that I'm not even there for her because it's like she is going through this shit all alone. Luckily, they haven't caught her with her phone, so we can still text because and she can call me once a day for fifteen minutes.

"Hey, you want to hang tonight?" One of my room-mates, Tia, asked in her thick, country accent.

"Naw, I think I'm gon' just chill tonight," I replied, already knowing that I'm going to have to hear her mouth.

She's cool and I've kicked it with her and some of her friends a few times, but I'm not the type that is going to be out every weekend. I never been that girl and ain't trying to be now. I'm just trying to keep my grades up and make it through this first semester. I still talk to Joy every other day and her and my momma still aren't speaking to each other. Just when I thought that I could finally get away from my momma and live my life the way that I wanted too, she ruined that. On the way down here to drop me off, she told me that she had an interview the following day down here.

She lives about forty minutes away from campus. We don't usually talk and when I do answer her calls, all she wants to do is trip about the fact that I haven't been answering her calls. Ever since I found out the truth about my dad's death, I haven't had much to say to my mom. I had to ride with her down here and she wasn't going to let me go to orientation without her. I have never even tried to talk to her about it because I know that as soon as I bring up my dad's name, the conversation is going to be over. I've texted with my aunt Mikki a few times, but I haven't really talked to her either.

"You don't have any homework and you're not going to be doing anything but sitting in this room being boring. You need to come with us," Tia begged.

Turning around in my computer chair to face her as she made this sad ass face, I gave in and told her that I would come. I got up to look in my closet to find something to wear when my phone started ringing. Snatching up the black dress that I decided on and everything else I needed, I made my way into the bathroom. Answering Cina's call, I silently prayed that things get better for her soon.

"Hey, Cee! How are you feeling?" I asked while turning on the shower to get it hot.

"Hey, Meria. I'm good, just tired as hell. I wish you

were here, but I got some good news today," Cina replied, happy as hell, catching me off guard.

"Girl, tell me, shit! I ain't heard you this happy in months."

"They are letting me the fuck out of here. Taniece reached out to my aunt Moe and she agreed to let me move with her. I'm not really moving with that bitch, but to get out this bitch, I'll tell them whatever they want to hear," Cee said, making sure to lower her voice saying the last part.

"Bitch, yessss! I'm happy as hell that you are getting the fuck out of there," I replied happier than her.

As Cina and I had our daily talk, I couldn't help but miss being able to be with each other every day. When I was at home, Cina was the first person that I talked to when I woke up and her annoying ass would be on the phone with me before I fell asleep. Our friendship has been the only constant friendship in my life. As much as we get on each other's nerves and damn sure don't agree on everything, bet not nobody else fix they mouth to say anything bad about one of o us to the other or be ready to fight.

"Have you heard anything about Chaos?" I asked.

"Yea, they keep postponing his court date. It's a bunch of bullshit, but hopefully he'll go to court next week. I just want him to be out. I'm so sick of this shit and not being able to talk to him makes it even harder," Cina admitted, and I could hear the fear of the unknown in her voice.

"It's going to all work out, and he'll be home before you know it."

Cina didn't reply to my last comment. She changed

the subject, and we had small talk for the remainder of the call. By the time I got off the phone with Cina, the water was finally hot. It's a few things that I miss about home and having hot water is damn sure one of them. College is cool, but sharing a room is not what I thought it would be like. I'm going to have to figure something out for next semester because this isn't going to work. Jumping in the shower, I got myself together before Tia started harassing me, thinking I'm not going to go out.

As Yo Gotti's *Put A Date On it* boomed through the speakers, I nodded my head and rapped along. Tia tapped me, trying to get my attention. Her drunk ass been getting on my nerves ever since we got here, but I'm trying to enjoy my night because who knows when I'll come out again. The liquor was starting to hit me. I was starting to get hot as I finished my last shot for the night.

"Sameria, you see him over there? The light skinned one," Tia whispered and pointed in the direction of three niggas and the light skinned one was staring right at me.

Quickly looking away, I checked my phone to see that Cina texted me, so I quickly texted her back. This drunk bitch been trying to get with every nigga that she seen tonight, so this is just another one. I didn't even waste my time saying anything about the nigga. He cute or whatever, but I've seen better. Looking up from my phone, I was surprised when the light skin nigga from across the room was now on the left of me and Tia was on the right.

"Sameria, this is my cousin Yasir. Yasir, this is my

roommate Sameria," Tia said, introducing us to each other and rushing away to the bar.

"Where you from? I know you ain't from 'round here," Yasir asked, looking me up and down.

"Denver," I replied and pulled out my phone, trying to get him to get out my face.

Tia made her way back over to where Yasir and I were now sitting. No matter how hard I tried to get this nigga away from me, he is not giving up. I'm barely answering his questions, and I know he can tell by my tone and my half ass answers I'm not interested. I whispered for Tia to get her fucking cousin out my face, but this drunk bitch just kept saying *huh*.

"I'm 'bout to go," I said, trying to get Yasir the fuck away from me.

"We should go get—" Yasir attempted to say before I cut him off.

"I ain't trying to be mean, but I'm not interested. It's plenty of bitches in here that will go wit' you wherever you're trying to take 'em," I scolded.

"Damn, for real, that's how you feel?" Yasir asked.

"Yea," I replied, brushing past him around the booth and making my way across the room to the bathroom.

I'm not looking for a nigga. Right now, all I want to do is focus on me. School is my only priority and everything else is taking the back burner. Getting into a position, so that I can take care of myself is all I care about. I've been holding on tight to the money that I got as gifts for graduation, the money Joy gave me before I left and the money that I had saved up so I wouldn't have to call and ask my mom for anything. It hasn't been easy, but I've managed to make it so far. I know that I'm soon going to have to get a job, which is going to make my time even shorter, but I'd rather do that than ask my mom for anything.

"Sameria, my cousin is trying to see what's up with you. Girl, he got money. Why are you actin' like that?" Tia asked with an attitude as she walked into the bathroom.

"Girl, I don't care about how much money yo' cousin got," I admitted as I walked out the bathroom stall.

Tia said some shit under her breath that I couldn't hear, and that was probably best. I called an Uber for us, and we made our way outside. As we waited outside for the Uber and Tia tried to sober up, here come her fucking cousin again, pulling up to where we are standing. Tia's eyes lit up, and I was just trying to figure out why because nobody is this damn happy about seeing their cousin. Then I recognized the nigga in the passenger side is the same nigga in the pictures that Tia has on her side of the room. Tia talks about this nigga Duck all the time. He used to be her boyfriend but not only did this nigga leave her, he left her for her best friend. The way that Tia is all up in his face, you would think that this wasn't the same nigga that not only played her ass but had her looking dumb as hell. Come to find out, he was fucking her best friend the whole year they were together. He wouldn't be able to say shit to me, let alone would I be happy to see him now. Cina stopped texting me back, so she must have fallen asleep.

"I can take y'all back to the campus," Yasir suggested.

"Naw, I'm good," I replied, and of course Tia opposed since she wanted to be around Duck any way she can.

Her cousin just gon' let her continue to be a dumb bitch, but my cousins wouldn't let me be on no bullshit like that. Not only would they tell me exactly what the fuck was up, they would let they niggas know that playing with me wasn't an option. I can already tell how they family rocks. Yasir jumped out his car and the people behind him were mad as hell that he's holding up traffic.

"I'll take you straight home. I don't need a kidnapping charge," Yasir said as he got up close enough to me that he invaded my space.

As close as Yasir is to me and with the street light shining down on us, I got to see him real good. The darkness in the club did nothing for him; he is fine. He smells good as hell in the Acua Di Gio cologne that Zion used to wear. Memories that we shared started to come to my mind, but I pushed them to the back because he damn sure ain't thinking about me.

Yasir stands about 6'0 hovering over me. Yasir has light skin, smooth and clear and some thick juicy lips. He's dressed head to toe in Gucci, turning heads and has a lot of attention on him. I can tell by the way bitches are calling his name and speaking as they walk by what he's all about.

"Straight to the campus," I replied, finally giving in.

"Straight there."

"Aye, Duck, hop in the back," Yasir instructed.

I can tell by the look on Duck's face and the way he sucked his teeth like a bitch that he didn't want to get in the back, but he got back there. You would have thought that Tia's drunk ass had hit the lottery as happy as she was. Her light skin was flushed, and her cheeks were rosy red from all the two dollars shots that she enjoyed. Yasir made sure that I was in the car good and made his way over to the driver side of the car.

"What the fuck! Muthafucka go!"

"You holdin' up fuckin' traffic! I got somewhere to fuckin' be."

"Hurry the fuck up!" People screamed from behind us, but Yasir didn't seem fazed and still took his time before pulling off.

This nigga definitely hustles. I can tell by his demeanor and the way he doesn't give a fuck that is his occupation. After Yasir got in the car, he stared at me so long that he damn near made me uncomfortable. I cocked my head to the side and rolled my eyes. Then he smiled and pulled off. He drove and as he tried to have small talk, I turned up his music because I wasn't interested. Right now, I don't have time for a nigga because the drama and bullshit I'm not about to put up with. Even when I think the niggas are different, they end up all being the same.

After about thirty minutes, we finally made it through the traffic and back to the campus. Before Yasir could stop the car good, I said, "Bye."

As I jumped out the car, I saw Tia's hoe ass in the back seat sucking dick. What the fuck type of cousin is Yasir? No matter how old I get, my cousin ain't having that shit. This hoe doing this now, she'll be blowing up this nigga's phone tomorrow and he'll have her ass blocked until he wants to be bothered. Shaking my head, Yasir jumped out the car and came after me.

"Look, I'm not gon' waste yo' time. I'm not playin' hard to get. I'm not interested. The last thing I need is a nigga that's in the streets all day and night fucking four to five bitches, in and out of jail. It's some bitches out there and that's what they want, but that bitch ain't me. I'm not impressed by the car or yo' muthafuckin' watch," I spat. I know it sounded harsh, but it is what it is.

"You got the wrong idea about a nigga. Yea, I used to be in the streets, but I don't do that shit no more. I flip houses, and I own a few businesses. A nigga got to be moving weight to drive a nice car and have a nice watch? I don't know what type of niggas you used to fuckin' wit', but I know how to get money in a whole lot of ways," Yasir said with confidence drippin' from his words.

"That's cool and all, but —" I attempted to say but Yasir cut me off.

"Just give me a chance. Let me show you because a nigga can tell you anything. Baby, I don't want nothin' from you," Yasir damn near begged and pulled me with one arm, wrapping his arm around my waist.

Snatching away, my pussy started getting moist. "Breakfast in the morning," I said and turned to leave.

"Cool, I'll pick you up at noon and take you to —" Yasir attempted to say.

"Naw, big money. You'll meet me at the Waffle House up the road at nine," I interjected and made my way to my dorm.

I'm not impressed by fancy restaurants and niggas spending money on me. I can't do nothin' with that shit. What impresses me is a nigga putting in time and being there. This ain't goin' nowhere. But after looking on Facebook and seeing that Zion is in a relationship with some bitch named Jacquee, I don't have shit to lose because he damn sure ain't coming back for me like I secretly hoped he would. I know the role I played in that situation, but the fact that he didn't even bother to come and see me off to college like he promised he would, I don't think that

I'll ever forgive that. If nothing else, Yasir can keep my mind of Zion because love is the last thing on my mind.

My feet were killing me. Soon as I got to the door of my room, I came up out of my shoes. I heard Tia's drunk ass calling my name as I walked up the walkway. I'm not taking care of no dumb drunk bitches today, so she's on her own. Our roommate, Ashlee, must be with her nigga because I haven't seen her since Biology class this morning. Me and Tia could never be more than roommates because the way that she moves just ain't how I do.

The crazy thing is that Tia comes from money; both her parents are successful realtors. She's spoiled as hell and whatever she wants, she gets. Grew up in the suburbs and has never even been to the hood, I recently learned, but she reminds me of so many of the bitches that I know back home from my hood. Brushing my teeth, I jumped in the shower. Tia was in the room because I could hear her drunk ass falling into shit. I wish she would have gone with that nigga Duck because I'm not trying to deal with this shit tonight. I got out the shower and wrapped my hair.

I slipped on some shorts and a t-shirt then made my way out the bathroom, so I can go to bed. I acted like I didn't even see Tia's drunk ass on the floor. I got right in my bed and put my sleep mask over my eyes so when this drunk bitch manages to get up, the light doesn't irritate me. This semester needs to hurry up and be over because I don't think I can handle too much of this. I don't care about her partying every day but damn, learn to hold yo' liquor and have some respect for yo'self.

"Sameria," Tia faintly said, and I buried my head in my pillow just like I didn't hear the bitch.

"So, this is what I have to do to be able to talk to yo' yellow ass and make sure that you're okay?" My mom attempted to whisper, but I know everybody that was out here heard her.

"Naw, momma, I been meaning to call you," I lied as I hugged Tasia.

I'm not even gon' lie, I miss Taisa. I'm so used to being with her every day. My mom not being willing to talk to me about my dad doesn't sit right with me, especially if what his momma said is true. My mom caught me coming out of my dorm room. I'd just finished my last class of the day and Yasir was here to pick me up for dinner. It's been two weeks since we met at the club and no matter how hard I pushed back trying to get him to give up, he hasn't. My momma poppin' up here damn sure wasn't in my plans for my night.

"What, you done met some nigga down here? Is that why I haven't heard from you? The least ya yellow ass could do is text me back and let me know that you're okay. You know that girls get snatched up every damn day, and I know you think you grown now, but I'm still yo' momma. I made all this possible by myself with no help," my mom scolded.

"Well my dad's family could have helped. If wouldn't have helped Jamar set up my dad." I said as my phone started vibrating in my back pocket.

"Tasia, go get a soda," my mom told Tasia but was muggin' me.

Pulling out my phone, it's Yasir asking me where I'm at. I quickly slipped my phone back into my picket and gave my attention back to my momma. The look that she was giving, I've seen too many times to count. Whenever I bring up my dad, I get this look. I already know that she's irritated and doesn't feel that she has to explain herself to me. I know that she wants to know where I got my information from, but she is too shocked to ask any questions.

"Sameria!" Yasir called out from behind me.

"I knew it was a nigga," my momma said. By the look she was giving me, she still had questions.

"What you doin'?" Yasir asked as he got up to me and my momma.

"I'm sorry, who are you?" My momma asked, demanding an answer.

Yasir looked at her crazy, and I let him know that she's my mom. His attitude switched up quick, and he got to talking like he was meeting with one of his clients about a house. He started referring to her as ma'am, asking her how she was doing and some more shit. I've heard the way that he talks to clients and white people, and he definitely has on his white people voice right now.

"You look too damn old to go here. How old are you?" My mom scolded.

"I'm twenty-five ma'am," Yasir replied.

"My daughter is only sixteen. What the fuck could yo' old ass want with her? Where did y'all meet?" My momma questioned, embarrassing the fuck out of me.

"I met Sameria through my cousin Tia," Yasir answered, looking over at me crazy.

I told him that I was eighteen, and I didn't think anything of it. Shit, I didn't think that we would still be talking now. All he had to say to win my momma over was that he was Tia's cousin because she loves Tia. When we met Tia and her family, my momma was convinced that I needed friends like Tia. Because she came from such a good upbringing and was so smart, she would be a great friend to have. She has no idea about the real Tia and how the bitch ain't been to class all week. She been in her feelings because she hasn't heard from Duck since the night she sucked him up on the way back from the club. Her parents been blowing her phone up and this bitch just been going out every night, hoping she'll run into Duck again.

"Pumpkin!" I yelled, so she could hear me downstairs.

"What the fuck are you screaming for? I'm right next door in my baby's room. When the fuck does Sameria get here? I'm sick of yo' ass," Pumpkin responded, not holding back her true feelings.

"She'll be here tomorrow. I was just trying to tell you that we need to be leaving soon, so we can make it to court on time."

"Alright, bring yo' big ass on."

I'm so happy to be back in the place that Chaos got for us. R'Shad kept paying the bills, so everything is just how we left it. My daughter will be here soon, but the only thing that is missing is her dad. I just wish that he could come home. I have to go to court today, but they can't know that I'm in communication with Pumpkin or any of Chao's family because of his pending charges. I just pray that today this shit comes to an end and they let him come home with us.

I made my way downstairs, and I had to stop to catch

my breath. Pumpkin didn't even wait for me, and she's outside honking the horn like I'm taking too long for her. Snatching up my purse, I made my way out the house and over to Pumpkin's car. I can't wait for Sameria to get here, I miss her so much. She's coming because Pumpkin is insisting that I have a baby shower, so they planned everything out together. Sameria hasn't been gone long, but it feels like forever. I know that I be getting on hers and that nigga she fucking with nerves, but I don't care. She's supposed to be here for me while I'm going through this.

"Did you ask R'Shad to pick up Sameria from the airport?" Pumpkin asked.

"Naw, I'm going to—" I attempted to answer before Pumpkin cut me straight the fuck off.

"What the fuck did the doctor tell yo' ass yesterday?"

"She just told me that I need to get more rest and relax. She didn't say that I couldn't leave the house. I'm already cutting back on not going to the shop, what else am I supposed to do?" I complained.

Nobody understands how hard it is to go through this shit by myself. Making money and staying busy is the only thing that is helping me to deal with this shit. Pumpkin has been coming by to check on me every day, and R'Shad makes sure that I'm good and all the bills are paid, but sitting in the house by myself and not having anybody there with me is not helping lower my stress. I'm already nervous about having my daughter, nobody gets that though. These are the times that I wish me and my momma had a good relationship, and she could be here to guide me through this.

I miss my little brother so much, but since I'm out

that group home, I can call him every day. My auntie Moe had no problem with lying and telling the state that I was living with her so she could get more assistance from em'. That bitch picked me up, signed the papers that she needed to sign, went and lied to the judge and dropped me off at our townhouse without an issue. You would think that she would call and check on me to make sure that I'm good, but the only time I hear from here is when she wants something from me.

We made it downtown in about twenty minutes, and Pumpkin pulled over on the side of the court house, so that I could get out and she can go find a parking spot. Caught up in my thoughts of my man finally being back home where he belongs, all I could do is pray that the judge sees the truth today. I got myself together and got out the car.

"Damn, hurry up. You always been slow in every way. Now you think you got an excuse but naw, that shit ain't sliding with me," Pumpkin commented over the lady laying on the horn behind her because she's holding up traffic.

As Pumpkin skirted off, I flicked off the lady that was behind her honking on the horn. My phone started ringing. It was Unique. She been acting weird, so I let her go to voicemail, so I can call Sameria. Unique kept trying to get with R'Shad and was on him hard, but he doesn't want her ass, so that's my fault. It ain't shit I can do about that. I called Sameria as I made my way over to the courthouse.

"What's up, Cina?" Yasir asked as the call connected.

"Damn, now you answering phones? I hope you paying Sprint too," I replied, serious as hell.

"Here go yo' girl."

"Damn, bitch! Niggas take you on a few dates, spend a few dollars and now you lettin' him answer the phone too. You fucked him, was it good?" I said as I sat down and checked the time.

"Shut up, I was in the shower. I told him to answer if you called because I wanted to know what happened at court. And yea, bitch, I did and bommmb," Sameria bragged.

"Finally, shit, it took long enough. I'm waiting to go in now. I'm nervous, Meria. I wish you were here already," I admitted.

"I know. I'm going to be there in the morning. Everything is going to be okay, but you need to relax. When you stress, the baby is feeling that shit too, Cee," Sameria nagged.

"I know and I'm trying not to, but what am I supposed to do? Everybody keep telling me what I need to do, but it's easier said than done because if I could do that shit then it would be done. I don't want to be stressing, but—"

"Ms. Miller, I'm glad you came. How are you feeling?" Taniece asked.

"Why are you here? I no longer have an open case," I asked irritated.

"I was subpoenaed by the court," Taniece replied, shrugging her shoulders, which let me know that shit is not about to go the way I want it to.

Promising Sameria I will call her as soon as I leave out of the courtroom, I got her off the phone and made my way in. Making my way through the metal detectors, I saw Felicia and R'Shad in the lane next. R'Shad nodded his head when he saw me, and Fe looked at me crazy. I don't know what that bitch's problem is, but she always got one. I just want that bitch to keep that same energy after I have my daughter because I been wanting to beat her ass for months.

As I rode up the elevator by myself, surrounded by people that I don't know, I started to feel a way that is starting to become too common; lonely. I never realized how attached to Ricardo I had become. He is my best friend, and I was with him everyday before all this shit happened. When I doubted myself and didn't think that I could do something, Ricardo was by my side making sure that I knew that I had shit on lock. During this time that he has been away, whenever I think about it, I can hear my momma's voice ringing in my head with all the bullshit that she has said about our relationship not lasting.

I made it down the long hallway to the courtroom, and as I walked in, they were bringing Ricardo into the court room. As he looked over at me, he smiled and I half smiled back, but seeing him in handcuffs and shackles just made me even sadder than I already am. I sat down on the opposite side of where all Ricardo's family was sitting. As the prosecutor talked, my stomach started to get tight and my daughter started kicking me hard as hell.

"The victim is here your honor," Ricardo's lawyer stated, looking back at me.

"Come on up, Ms. Miller," the Judge stated, motioning for me to come up to the podium.

The look on the judge and the prosecutor's face was sympathy for me and disgust whenever she looked at Ricardo as I walked over to the podium on Ricardo's side. The prosecutor already knew what it was. I answered all her questions and she kept asking me the same questions over and over. I felt like she was trying to pressure me into changing my story. She basically let me know that with or without my testimony, they were going to go forward with charges against Ricardo, even though he hadn't done shit to me. When I didn't fall for her shit, she seemed to have an attitude and rushed me out of her office.

"Your honor, I understand everything that defense is trying to say, but what it boils down to is the safety of the victim. We have sworn statements from her mother that states that she was being held against her will by the defendant. Him being released is not a good idea because we have to worry about the trauma that this may cause the victim, and she is pregnant. If you are going to release him, there needs to be a restraining order put in place," the prosecutor pleaded.

"Go ahead, Ms. Miller. Is there anything that you would like to say?" The judge asked.

"I'm not a victim, and I wish that y'all would quit referring to me as one. Ricardo needs to be home; our daughter will be here soon. This is not fair, he didn't do anything wrong. This is all because of some lies that my momma told y'all. Ask Taniece, the social worker that the courts put over my case with my mother since she had to be investigated because of the stuff that she was doing. Tell them Taniece. This isn't fair. Ricardo didn't do anything to me. Everything that y'all are accusing him of doing never happened," I said as I began to cry, looking back at Taniece.

The Judge asked Taniece to come up and one of Ricardo's lawyers guided me back over to my seat. I'm so sick of crying. Having to be so weak now is not something that I want to get used to. As Taniece started talking, I thought that she might help by telling the truth about my mom, but I was wrong as hell.

"Your honor, Rita Miller has been investigated by our department and we have found that there were several inconsistencies in her stories involving the relationship between Ricardo and Cina, but with our findings, we also feel that there may need to be some protection put in place for Cina," Taniece stated as I stared her down.

"I don't need no fucking protection!" I spat losing it and fed up with all this bullshit.

"Ms. Miller, I'm going to have to ask you to be quiet, or I'm going to have to ask you to leave if you can't control yourself." The judge demanded.

"Can we please approach?" The prosecutor asked in between whispering to the other lady that's working with her.

"Yes. Ms. Washington, approach as well," the judge said, referring to Taniece.

Resting my hands on my stomach and looking over at Pumpkin and R'Shad, I don't know which one was madder. I'm honestly surprised that neither one of them haven't said anything. Every time Pumpkin comes to court, the judge threatens to kick her out. And I've never seen R'Shad this quiet, especially not with them talking about his brother. I don't even know why Felicia is here, Ricardo doesn't fuck with her like that, and she hasn't looked up from her phone since I walked in the courtroom.

"It seems that there we have all been able to reach an agreement that Ricardo needs to be released and placed on pre-trial. The court is ordering a GPS electronic monitoring. Also, I am ordering that restraining order be put in place to make sure that the victim, whether she likes it or not, is protected during this process. So, a restraining order is going to be put in place, a temporary one that lasts for —" the judge stated. I jumped up with my phone to my ear so that I can call Sameria.

"This is some bullshit!" I screamed and made my way out the court room.

"Bitch, get up!" Sameria screamed as I rolled over for the hundredth time trying to get comfortable, but that just isn't happening.

"R'Shad should have made yo' ass stand outside until I woke up. Who comes in somebody's house at this time of the morning screaming?" I stated as Sameria jumped on my bed.

"I should have caught an Uber because he was threatening to put me out his car the whole way here. I can't stand his ass. Bitch, you call me every day saying that you wish I was here, and now I'm here, so bitch, get up. Staying in the bed isn't going to change the situation. It's fucked up, I know, but you know that Chaos loves you. This isn't something that is going to last forever. They can't keep y'all apart for too much longer.

Tomorrow is your big day and if you don't enjoy this, you're going to end up regretting it. This is our first baby, and we need to make memories celebrating this. I know that it hasn't been easy, Cee, but this is why me and Pumpkin both have gone through all of this putting it together. Bitch, I could have stayed in Texas if you were gon' be acting stank, layin' in bed and shit. Huh, hoe. Get up and wash yo' ass, so we can make sure everything is how you want it to be," Sameria demanded, tossing a flip phone at me.

It started ringing and I answered it. "Cee!" Ricardo screamed into the phone as the call connected. I hadn't heard his voice in so long, I couldn't help but smile. All the words that I've been wanting to say were caught in my throat as Ricardo started telling me how much he missed me. Tears started falling so fast and it wasn't because I was sad for once. Hearing his voice after over a month means a lot but call me selfish. I want him here with me right now, fuck the police!

"I miss you so much. I can't wait until this shit is over and you can come home," I commented and couldn't help but smile from ear to ear.

"Damn, I can hear you smiling through the phone and shit. Quit fucking crying, I already feel bad enough for the way shit is going. I ain't gon' lie, I miss you too. Why is yo' phone turned off? Pumpkin been trying to call you. And she came over there to try to give you that phone. It's fucked up that I can't be there, but I got you and Lilly."

"I'm not naming my baby Lilly. I don't know why you keep saying that. Can you just come over for a little bit?"

"I can't, Cee. If I could then I would already be over there. With me being on this fucking box, I can't even leave the house without permission. I'm on lock down, and I can't leave for sure for two weeks."

"How is this going to work? You're supposed to be there for the baby shower, when I go into labor and bring her home. This is not fair. Why the fuck is this happening? I swear my fuckin' momma put a curse on us!" I whined.

"Cina, I know that this shit isn't easy, and I know that it's been hard. How the fuck do you think I been? Because of yo' fucking momma lyin', I been locked up and missing out on shit with you that I can't get back. How the fuck do you think that makes a nigga feel? You not the only one that's going through this shit, Cina! Then that shit with yo' people. Why the fuck didn't you tell me?" Ricardo barked.

"So, you're trying to blame me for this shit? You think this is my fault?" I screamed so loud that my voice cracked.

"Quit yelling. That's not what I said. I'm just being honest and telling you what it is. Do you want me to lie to you?"

"Bet."

Click.

I thought that when we finally were able to talk that I would be so happy and nothing else would matter, but the way he just talked to me, I wasn't expecting. He's never talked to me so coldly. I understand that he's going through shit too because he's was locked up because of it, but don't make me feel like it's my fault. I knew that R'Shad was going to tell him about Lil Miller and my momma plotting, but I didn't think he would blame me.

"Bitch, what the fuck happened?" Sameria asked, snatching the covers off me, trying to pry my hands off my face.

"My mom was right. It's not going to last. He's going to be done with me because of that shit with Lil Miller. I didn't tell him because I knew that he would feel a way.

Why would he even bring that up right now? Clearly, I was on his side or I would have set shit up for them to get him," I cried as Sameria hugged me and rubbed my back.

"I'll be right back," Sameria said. She jumped up from the bed and ran down the stairs.

"Y'all not about to get on my fucking nerves today. This is supposed to be a fucking celebration. Why y'all both acting like some bitches? If y'all can't make it through this little shit, y'all not gon' last. I understand that you feel alone, but bitch, you're not. I been over here every damn day. I'm not Ricardo, I'm not gon' be over here kissing yo ass. If you want me to show you what alone is, bitch, I can do that," Pumpkin said, standing in my bedroom doorway.

"I know that you're here for me, Pumpkin. I do appreciate everything that you do. But it's not fairr—"

"Girl, life ain't fair. How the fuck do you think Ricardo feels? Not only is he fighting a case, they are saying that he might not be able to see his daughter be born or even at all until this shit is worked out. You need to grow the fuck up. You're going to be a mom soon and this punk shit that you been on here lately is not going to work. Let yo' balls drop and get yo' ass up! Laying in that bed ain't gon' change shit, Cina. I know bitches that wish they had a piece of man like Ricardo, but yo' ass sittin' here naggin' him about shit that he can't control. I ain't saying it's yo' fault, but yo' ass should have told us what the fuck yo' people were plotting and planning!" Pumpkin spat and stormed away.

Moving the covers, I found the flip phone and went to the call log, so I can call Ricardo back. Before I could, he called. Taking a deep breath and trying to calm down, I answered the phone. I know this isn't going to be easy and it is really going to put our relationship to the test, but I know that we can make it through this. I didn't say anything as the call connected, I just breathed hard into the phone.

"Cee, I'm gon' keep it a hundred with you. This arguing shit, you already know I don't do that. I'm not about to fight with you. We're supposed to be fighting this shit together with these other muthafuckas, not beefin' with each other."

"I know, but I feel like you are blaming me for all this happening. I couldn't tell you about what was goin' on. That is the main reason why I kept going back to Rita's so I would know what was going on, and I could keep anything from happening to you."

"Look Cee, I hear you, but you should have told me. Shit could have went left. Cee, no matter what, we need to always tell each other what the fuck is going on. Anything else makes me question if you really down with a nigga."

"What are we going to do? How is this going to work?"

As Chaos and I talked, Sameria came back into the room pulling me by my arm, making me get out the bed. Chaos assured me that everything was going to be okay. I know that sometimes I overreact, and I know that he has my back, willing to do whatever to make sure that I'm good. He's showed me time and time again that no matter what, he'll never switch up on me.

I'm not gon' lie, I don't know how the fuck this is going to work and the unknown is what worries me the most. I wish that things could be easier, but Pumpkin is right. We have to be willing to go through shit now to be able to make it. The more we talked, the more my nerves started to calm down. I have to take the good with the bad. At least we can talk to each other now. Shit, to be honest, he is risking his freedom by even talking to me.

"You take yo' last test today, don't you?" Ricardo asked.

"Yea, I'm nervous," I admitted.

"You got that shit."

Today I take my last test to complete my GED. It hasn't been easy, but I finally made it to this point. When I first started taking my tests, I thought it was going to be a lot harder than it was. With me finishing this, I can get ready to take my test so I can be a licensed nail tech. Once I do that, you ain't gon' be able to tell me shit and the price is definitely going up.

I grabbed a white, PINK shorts and matching shirt, so I can be comfortable while running around with Pumpkin and Sameria. Ricardo had to hang up because his case manager was at the door. I jumped in the shower because I could hear Sameria and Pumpkin talking shit downstairs. Sameria and Pumpkin picked out everything, and Pumpkin been talking shit through the whole process.

My phone started ringing. *I don't know who this is.* I answered and shortly after, I wished that I would have let the caller go to voicemail. I don't know how this bitch got my number, but my auntie is probably who gave in to her.

"So, you weren't going to invite me to the baby shower?" My mom taunted.

"No. Why would I invite you to my baby shower? Did you forget you're not supposed to have any communication with me?"

"How much money do you have? I need a few—"

"I don't care about what you need. Did you forget that I'm about to have a baby? That's my only concern. She's doing fine, thanks for asking."

"The baby is going to be retarded anyway."

"Fuck you! Don't call my phone again or I'm going to call the police and have yo' ass in jail."

"Bitch, I wish you would call the police on me."

Click.

I hate that shit has to be this way with me and my momma. Even though I said it, I would never fix my mouth to call the police on anybody, even her. After all the shit that she has put me through, I still wish that she would change so that we could have some type of relationship. But that will never happen and one day, I'll just have to accept that.

"Cina, for real, hurry up! We need to be leaving soon!" Sameria screamed upstairs.

"Alright!"

Brushing my teeth, I waited for the shower to get hot. I jumped in the shower and just threw my hair in a ponytail. Slipping into my PINK slides because my feet are swollen, I made my way downstairs. I love when Pumpkin is here because she always cooks. I know how to cook, but if I don't have to, I damn sure appreciate it.

"Why are you still here? Go home. I'm sure yo' bitch is looking for you," Sameria complained.

"Because I don't have to. What, you mad because that nigga Zion don't want you?" R'Shad said and started laughing, but he was serious as fuck.

"Nigga, please don't think I'm pressed about Zion. I can show my call log that shows whose pressed," Sameria bragged.

"Don't think that means yo' pussy fire because it's not."

"Come on, I got shit to do other than this damn baby shower. Ain't yo' appointment at noon for yo' test?" Pumpkin complained.

22

SAMERIA

"I want you to be with Scar. That way you'll move back home," Cina whined.

"Bitch, please. I'm good where I'm at," I said as we walked around the venue that we rented for the baby shower.

Everything was being set up just how we asked. Cina was happy and it's not even complete yet. They have a few more hours before everything is supposed to be done and the way that Pumpkin is cutting into them, that should get them to moving faster. Even though Cina hasn't said anything today, I know that she wishes that her momma was here. Her mom wasn't always scandalous like she is now. They used to be close when we were kids, but when Cina's dad left, all that changed.

"You like him doe, and he definitely likes yo' ass. From what I heard, him and Felicia ain't working out."

"Bitch, I don't care. I do not want Scar. I got a man," I said with emphasis on *man*.

"Since when? Today? Because you been saying that

he's just yo' friend. I knew yo' ass was lying. *I ain't lookin'
for no nigga, I just want somebody that I can kick it with
when I ain't in class. I'm just trying to make it through school
and get in a position to make sure I'm good without my
momma's help.* Blah, blah, blah. I knew y'o ass was just
talking. So, what happened? That nigga fucked you so
good that he made you change yo' mind?" Cina
predicted.

"Fuck you! Naw, bitch, that ain't what happened.
He's different and he's not like all these other niggas.
He's a man, and I didn't know before, but it's a big
difference. He told me the night that I met him that he
didn't want anything from me. It's been over a months,
and he hasn't switched up. I'm not gon' lie, for a minute
I was just waiting for some bullshit to happen, a bitch
to pop up or something, but nothing has happened. He
understands and respects my schedule. He's not
running the streets or running from the police and shit.
Bitch, he has his own business. Bitch, and my momma
like him."

"Yo' momma like him? She doesn't like no damn body.
Bitch, she don't even like you most days. So, he's old like
my paw-paw old, right?" Cina asked, trying to be funny. I
flicked her off and walked away.

Cina, Pumpkin and I finished walking around,
making sure things were being done correctly. This has to
be perfect. Cina hasn't been able to enjoy her pregnancy.
Back to back it seems like she is always dealing with some
bullshit. I'm going to make sure that this is perfect and
anybody that tries to fuck this is up is going to have to see
me. She deserves to enjoy the rest of her pregnancy with
no drama.

"Is it anything that you want different? Or anything that you want that you don't see, Cee?" I asked.

"Naw, I love everything. I'm glad it's not pink because you know that I don't fuck with pink."

"Pumpkin wanted it to be pink, but I told her that I would have had to fight yo' ass if you came in here and seen a bunch of pink shit. Cee, you are having a girl. You not gon' let her wear nothing pink? You know people are going to bring her pink shit, right?"

"I'll smile, say thank you and pack it up for somebody to give away. My baby is not going to wear pink."

I rolled my eyes and we made our way over to talk the party planner that Pumpkin was cutting into about the centerpieces on the family tables. We didn't have much time to put this together, but I have to say, everything came together just like I envisioned. My phone started vibrating and it was a text message from Yasir. I couldn't help but smile and I hadn't even opened the message.

It's something about him that I can't get enough of. When he found out my real age, I just knew that he was gon' be done with me, but he wasn't. My momma talked hella shit and Cina always got jokes, but we're good. Age ain't nothing but a number, and I'm seventeen now. And in no time, I'll be eighteen.

"Bitch, I ain't never seen you smiling like this. Hoe, and you getting thick," Cina's irritating ass commented.

"Shut up."

"Let me see what the invitations that you sent out look like. I hope you didn't invite nobody I don't like."

"Where is Nique?" I asked, handing her one of the invitations.

"I ain't talked to Nique. She claimed she was coming

over last night, but she never showed up. I don't have time for some timey bitches. She been acting funny and then when she does come around, she on some gimmie shit. I don't have nothing to give to nobody, and she always got her hands out asking. I told her that she needs to get some money from all the niggas she out there fucking. How is she fucking all these niggas and can't call none of em' to get a few dollars?"

"That's yo' cousin."

"You know how I feel about blood. She claim she comin' to the shower doe."

"Did you invite yo' dad's sister?"

"Yea, but I don't know if she is coming. Mi-Mi felt a way when I got in contact with her to tell her to stop giving Rita money because she lost custody of me. She wanted me to come and stay with her, but I don't really even know her like that. All I know is that she been sending me money. But why now does she want to be a part of my life? I'm not living with nobody but Chaos."

"You need to stop being so damn mean."

"Why didn't that old man come with you up here?" Cina asked, waiting for an answer.

"Shut up, he's not that old. He had business that he had to take care of."

"Well, I need to meet Paw-Paw because he needs to know that if he does anything to you that I'm coming for him and that's on me."

"You'll meet him soon," I assured her.

I don't know how things got to where they are at with me and Yasir. His persistence for one, showed me that he was willing to put into work to get me. It wasn't just something that he was doing just to do because every time I was with him, it was evident that females were not something that were hard to come by for him. Yasir will sit in the library with me for hours, and he's even helped me study. I can talk to him about everything; he knows all my dreams and knows what it takes to make me smile. The fact that there is no drama in our relationship is what means the most to me.

Having somebody that fucks with me how I fuck with them is something that I never had before until I met Yasir. It's not perfect and he does way more partying than I like but other than that I can't complain. The way he is there for me I've never had before and it's not because of what he can do for me. It's about the time that he puts in and how he cares for me. Once he got me he didn't change and stop doing all the things that got me in the first place.

"WHAT ARE YOU DOING HERE?" I asked as I rubbed my eyes, fighting my sleep.

"None of yo' fucking business. You don't pay no bills here. Take yo' ass back to Texas," R'Shad spat. I flicked him off and made my way downstairs.

I'm glad he's over here putting together the rest of the baby's stuff because I damn sure ain't trying to do that. When we made it back to the house, Cina fell asleep, and she's been sleep for hours. Her ass ain't getting up no time soon. With the party planner handling everything, all we have to do is relax and show up tomorrow. I'm bored. I called Unique and texted her, but she hasn't responded. Joy is at work, but she's coming to the shower, so I'll see her then.

Zion has been calling me, but I don't have anything to say. He has a bitch and I have a man, so he made his decision and I made mine. It's best that we just keep it at that. I know somebody probably told him that I was in town because muthafuckas love to run they mouth. He had been calling me since the night I met Yasir like he knew I was moving forward.

"That boy was just asking about you," Pumpkin said as I walked in the kitchen.

"Who?" I asked, already knowing the answer.

"The one that used to hang with R'Shad and Ricardo," Pumpkin replied.

"That nigga doesn't fuckin' hang with me," R'Shad commented as he walked into the kitchen.

"Well, when I ran by the house, he was over there with Ricardo and he asked me were you over here. I told him I didn't know. I'm not the fucking love connection," Pumpkin said as she finished fixing her plate and made her way out the kitchen.

I ran upstairs to get my phone off the charger, and R'Shad tried to trip me as I walked past him. "Bitches love running behind niggas who really don't give a fuck about 'em," R' Shad commented. I didn't waste my time responding.

I ran to the guestroom, snatched my phone up and tried to call Zion back. I told myself that if he didn't answer then I would just leave it alone. He didn't answer, so I made my way downstairs, so I could eat. I sat in the living room with Pumpkin, and we caught up on everything that's been going on since I been gone. I knew a lot of it because Cina and I talk so much, but I just listened. About an hour passed, and R'Shad came running down the stairs screaming into the phone.

"I don't want to hear none of that shit you talkin' 'bout. I already told you what the fuck it was, but you think that because of the history we got that I'm gon' keep dealing with this shit. Like the fuck I said, Fe—" R'Shad screamed as he went out the front door slamming it, causing the windows to shake.

"I'm so sick of that bitch," Pumpkin said, shaking her head.

A few minutes later, the doorbell rang. I jumped up to answer it. I don't know who it could be. This bitch always on my case about no new friends, so it better not be some new friends. It was Unique. As red as her eyes are and the weed and liquor that I could smell on her like it's perfume, I can tell she's faded. Her rosy cheeks show me that.

"Hey bitch, welcome home," Unique said with her words slurred.

"Hey, Cee is sleep," I said. By my tone and the way her facial expression changed, I know that she could hear my attitude.

"And she's my cousin and this is her house," Unique replied, returning the attitude as I moved over so she could come in. She fell as she went to walk past me.

"Drunk ass," I said as I went to close the door but couldn't because somebody put their foot in the door preventing me.

"You can take yo' ass somewhere else with all that shit. Like Sameria told you, Cina is sleep and all yo' ass want is to come over here begging for something," Pumpkin spat as she helped Unique off the floor.

"Damn, you gon' close the door on me?" Zion said as I opened the door back up.

"Why are you here?"

"I was giving Unique a ride over here. I ran into her at Pumpkin's," Zion tried to explain.

"Well, bye," I said, trying to close the door.

"Just come talk to me right quick," Zion begged and started pulling my arm, closing the front door behind me.

"Let go of me!" I said, snatching away from his grasp.

Zion smells good and he looks even better, no matter how irritated I am with the way things turned out between us. I could have possibly handled shit differently than I did at my graduation party, but he also should have put his baby momma in her place way before he did. It wasn't meant to be. What's done is done and there is no way that we can take anything back. The breeze felt good and I'm glad because earlier it was hot as hell.

"What do you want, Zion?" I asked, breaking the silence as we sat on the steps in front of the house.

"Do you miss me?" Zion asked as he hugged me from the back.

"Naw, yo' girl probably looking for you doe," I shot back, looking back at him.

"I don't have no girl. I know you probably referring to that shit on Facebook. I can't control what a bitch post on there. You know I don't even do none of that shit. I kicked it wit' the bitch a few times. We went and got something to eat and went to the fuckin' movies, nothing special," Zion claimed.

"It doesn't matter."

"Why doesn't it matter? Are you fucking with some-body down there?" Zion asked and his whole demeanor changed, waiting for an answer.

"You didn't even come and see me before I left. You don't care because if you did, you would have been there," I admitted.

"Are you for real? Yo' momma didn't tell you that I came by. She told me that you weren't there. I knew that she was lying, but what the fuck was I supposed to do, argue with yo' momma? I told you that I fucked up, and I was willing to make shit right. Even if yo' momma didn't tell you, I know that you got my phone calls and texts. A nigga been blowing you up and yo' ass can't take time out yo' day to even respond."

"My momma didn't tell me that you came by. But all—"

"You quick to bring up the shit that I did wrong, but remember you was the one hollering that you didn't want a relationship. You were going off to college and this and that, but you quick to make it seem like the way that shit played out was my fault."

I didn't respond. I just laid back as Zion and I continued to talk. I was being childish ignoring him. And since I was the one being persistent that I didn't want a relationship, I really shouldn't have tripped about how he was handling his baby momma. Before anything, Zion was my friend, and I miss our friendship no matter how many times I say that it doesn't matter.

"I know you fucking with somebody. You love him?" Zion asked.

"Why?" I asked as I broke our embrace and went to

stand up and face him, but Zion pulled me down on his lap.

I don't love Yasir, but that's not none of his business. I shouldn't have called him back. I should have just left it alone. I shouldn't have put myself in this position. The way he is looking at me is making me think about the good times that we had.

"Can I just get tonight? After that, I'll leave you alone. But if you ever need a nigga, you can always call. I don't give a fuck what I'm doing or what I got going on, I'll drop it for you, Sameria," Zion pleaded as he rubbed my back with one hand and caressed my thigh with the other.

"I don't know about tha—"

Before I could finish my sentence, Zion wasted no time sliding his tongue in my mouth. As we kissed, feelings that I thought were gone all started to come back with the way that he is caressing my ass that is falling out the bottom of my shorts. I straddled his lap, not fucking up our kiss. Even though I know it may not be right, it feels right. We kissed and felt all over each other.

"Get the fuck off my brother's steps!" R' Shad spat from behind me, causing Zion to stop kissing me.

"I been trying to get at you, Scar," Zion said as I got off his lap.

"Nigga, it ain't shit you need to get at me about," Scar grunted and made his way in the house.

"Let's go," I said, grabbing Zion's hand and leading the way to his car.

23

CINA

"What are you doing here?" I asked in between yawns, waiting for Ricardo to answer.

"You been calling my brother complaining about needing this shit put together, right? So that's what the fuck I'm over here doing. I could still be in my bed, you ain't my baby momma," R'Shad spat, not evening looking up at me.

"Thanks, uncle Scar," I said and made my way downstairs because I could smell breakfast cooking.

I'm hungry as hell. Ricardo didn't answer, so he must still be sleep. I was surprised when I walked into the kitchen and Pumpkin was in here cooking. I just knew that it was Sameria. She stays talking shit, but whenever she's around, she always makes sure I eat good because she be cooking full course meals.

"Good morning," Pumpkin said as she breathed hard answering her phone.

"Good morning. Where's Sameria at?" I asked as the

alarm let me know that someone was opening the front door.

"Coming back from sucking dick," Pumpkin said.

I couldn't help but laugh. I was planning on taking a nap, I didn't think that I would sleep that long. I was supposed to take a nap and then get up, so me and Sameria could put together some more of the baby's stuff, but that didn't happen. Yoni should be here in a minute to do my hair and Kay-Kay should be here to do my make-up.

"Where you been?" I asked as Sameria tried to sneak up the backstairs quietly.

I turned around to face her and her hair was all over her head. I already knew what she was doing even without her answering. I couldn't help but laugh because she tried to sneak in like she was sneaking into to Susie's house. Sameria came back down the stairs, sat across from me on the island and went to grab a biscuit off the counter, but Pumpkin stopped that.

"Ut unn, I know that yo' momma raised you better than that. Who knows where the fuck yo' hands been? You been out sucking and fucking all night. Wash yo' fucking hands before you come in here touching anything," Pumpkin spat, smacking Sameria's hand.

"What about that old man? I thought he was the best man and all that other shit you were saying," I asked, impatiently waiting for an answer.

"I had been sitting with Pumpkin, drinking and smoking since yo' ass fell asleep on me. Zion popped up over here, one thing led to another and I ended up going with him. Nothing has changed, and I'm not leaving Yasir. We spent one night together and that was all it was."

"What do you think that old nigga is going to say about that?" I asked.

"You keep talking shit about her fucking with some old nigga. Are you fucking somebody from the nursing home you working at?" Pumpkin asked, causing all of us to bust out laughing.

We sat and talked while eating breakfast. I went and jumped in the shower before Yoni and Kay-Kay got here. I have two outfits that I'm going to wear. Pumpkin and Sameria talked me into wearing a dress even though I didn't want to, so I'm going to wear it for a few hours then I'm changing. I'm excited to see everything now that it's finished, but I wish that Ricardo could come.

As I made my way downstairs, I walked by the baby's room and R'Shad was still in there putting together my daughter's room. Me and Ricardo have to decide on a name because we don't have long. I could hear Yoni talking, so I know that she's here. I stopped to look at my daughter's room before making my way downstairs. R'Shad even hung up all of her clothes and organizing them by colors.

"Are you bringing Fe to the shower?" I asked.

"Yea, she's coming. This is the last thing I'm putting together. Y'all gon' have to figure something else out. I'll pay a crackhead to come do some shit if you need something else done, but this is it. I got other shit to do," R' Shad said as he got up dusting himself off.

"You did all this by yo'self?" I asked as I walked around the room.

"Yea, yo' girl was supposed to help, but she left with that fuck nigga Zion."

"Are you mad she went with him? What happened

with you and Zion? He was getting money with y'all not too long ago," I questioned.

"Hell naw, I ain't mad. Yea, he was, but then that nigga started acting like a bitch when Sameria left town. Business is business and if you can't do yo' job then I ain't fucking with you. I don't care who the fuck you are," R'Shad spat as my phone started ringing.

MY FEET WERE KILLING ME. Sneaking out the party, I made my way upstairs to our room. We're supposed to be staying here tonight at the hotel, but I think I just want to go home. Plopping down on one of the beds, I pulled my phone out now that I have a second without somebody in my face, trying to rub my stomach or take a picture. I'm trying to make the best out of this, but I just really wish that Ricardo was here.

Everything turned out perfect. Sameria and Pumpkin set up everything just how I wanted it to be. Putting a pillow under me, I laid back on my back and tried to call Ricardo. I was waiting for him to answer when Sameria came barging into the room. Just when I was about to hang up he answered. I know I'm about to hear her mouth, I just needed a break.

"Really, bitch?" Sameria asked.

"Meria, I needed a break, and I need to get out this fucking dress," I whined.

"Bitch, you got five minutes because everybody is looking for yo' ass," Sameria claimed.

"Did R'Shad put everything together?" Ricardo asked.

"It's a few more things that need to be put together, but he said he not putting nothing else together."

"I'll get Chuck to come over there and finish getting shit right," Ricardo said as he sat the phone down.

Chuck is one of Ricardo's customers, but that nigga does everything. He painted for us when we moved into our townhouse and moved all of our stuff. He fixes and details cars, and he'll hook up cable for you. It's not much that Chuck can't do and if he can't get it done, he'll get somebody that can. Chuck is cool, so I don't have an issue with him coming to the house and he's loyal to Ricardo, so we know that we won't have an issue with anybody finding out where we live.

Ricardo and I talked while Sameria texted her boo. My eyes were starting to get heavy. I would love to go to sleep, but I knew that I needed to get back to the party. Ricardo and I were going back and forth about names. Being able to talk to him whenever I want to after not being able to is making this distance between us a little easier.

"Alright, bitch, yo' time is up. Bro, she'll call you back!' Sameria said, snatching my phone.

Rolling my eyes and not putting up a fight, I jumped up and made my way to the bathroom, so I could change into something more comfortable. I hate dresses and these sandals that matched it were hurting my fucking feet. I changed my jewelry, so that it matched my blouse. I thought that Sameria had made her way back downstairs to the party until she started screaming my name.

"Bitch, why are you screaming? I'm coming," I said as I dragged myself out of the bathroom and back into the suite.

"I got a surprise for you downstairs come on," Sameria said, pulling my hand and dragging me out the room.

"If you ain't got a magical wand to get my baby daddy here, then bitch, nothing else is going to surprise me."

"You gon' be surprised by this. Nique, go and get em'," Sameria said as we walked back into the room where the party is being held.

Sameria covered up my eyes, taking this surprise shit overboard. I don't know what it could be but by the look on Sameria's, Nique and Pumpkin's faces, they think it's something that should make me happy. With everything I've been through lately, it takes a lot to get me excited because just when I think that shit is going to get better, that is when everything goes left.

"Look, Cee, yo' dad came," Sameria said as she removed her hands from my eyes, and I laid eyes on my father, Brian, but everybody calls him Brick.

"Awl hell naw!" Pumpkin screamed out, catching my attention and the bitch that is standing next to Brick.

"Baby girl," Brick said as he came closer to me, trying to hug me.

I shook my head and stepped back, giving him a warning not to get any closer. When I was younger, I prayed that my dad would show up and save me from Rita, but he never did. I never asked Rita what happened or why Brick left because I knew better than to question her. If he cared, he would have showed up way before now. I don't give a fuck about none of those gifts him or the bitch he with is holding. I'm sure she's the reason why he's been MIA all this time.

"Can we just talk," Brick asked, trying to reason with me.

"Yea," Sameria answered for me.

I scrunched up my face and followed behind Brick and Sameria out of the hall and into one of the hotel's lobbies. Even with my back turned, I already know the muthafuckas in here got something to say, but I don't care. I'm not about to pretend for none of them or Brick. His ass should have been there while I was dealing with Rita and her shit.

"I'm not trying to interrupt y'all family reunion, but me and this bitch right here have some unresolved issues," Pumpkin spat as she ran up on Brick's bitch, causing her to drop all the gifts.

Brick tried to stop them, but the way that Pumpkin was fucking up this lady, he was just trying not to get hit too. Sameria even tried to get Pumpkin off this bitch's head, but I don't think nobody is going to be able to stop this from happening. R'Shad ran into the lobby and broke up the fight, but Pumpkin did not stop willingly. She still kept swinging and talking hella shit.

"Bitch, every time I see you, remember that it's on sight. I don't give a fuck where we at, I'm beating yo' ass every time. On my sister's grave, hoe!" Pumpkin promised.

Looking over at Brick and his girl, her face was all fucked up. Her left eye was purple and blue. She came into the party with a long, freshly done weave and she leavin' out missing several tracks and her white halter dress is covered in her own blood. Shaking my head, Brick instructed his bitch to wait for him in the car, and she didn't put up a fight. She found her sandal that Pumpkin beat her ass out of and made her way out the hotel. She looked so scared, she didn't even look up. She kept her head pointed towards the ground.

"Look, Pumpkin, I'm sorry about that. If I would have known that you would be here, I wouldn't have brought her here," Brick said, looking back and forth between Pumpkin and me.

I sat down on a couch in the middle of the lobby and started texting Chaos. I don't know what the fuck that lady did to Pumpkin, but I know that it had to be something serious for her to act like this today. Sameria came and sat next to me, repeatedly apologized for inviting him here. It's not her fault, she had good intentions, but this wasn't the time for a family reunion. Too much time has passed and too much has happened for me to act like everything is all good because it's not.

"Cina, if I would have known shit was going to play out this way, I wouldn't have brought her here. Whatever happened between them, it doesn't have shit to do with us. I know that I haven't been here for you like I should have, but I want to make shit right now. I shouldn't have left you there, I was wrong. That money that my sister was giving Rita was from me and at the time, I couldn't come to you because I felt bad for all the time that had pass—" Brick attempted to say, and I cut him off.

"You think I give a fuck about that money? Rita didn't do shit for me with that money. When you left, my momma turned on me. You don't know what the fuck it was like. All the shit that I had to go through, and you think that you can just show up now and everything is supposed to be cool," I said.

I couldn't stop the tears from falling. Sameria hugged me and kept rubbing my back as I tried to catch my breath. Thinking about all the times my momma hit me... Where was he when I had to be in that group home? Where was he when I had to go to Pumpkin's just to be able to eat because Rita said I couldn't eat her food? The way that she talked to me and started treating me was right after Brick left. For years I tried to figure out why he left and didn't get anywhere. now with him sitting in front of me, I really don't know what else to say or how to feel. I feel he's too late.

"Cina, I know that I can't just show up and think that boom, just like that we're good. I want to explain to you what happened, the truth," Brick stated.

"And nigga, you thought this was the time?" Pumpkin asked.

"P, mind yo' business," R'Shad said, ushering her away.

"What happened?" I said, waiting for an answer.

Brick looked back and forth between me and Sameria a few times, causing us both to become confused. "It ain't no easy way to say this shit, but this is what it is. I found out that Rita helped Susie set up Sean, so I couldn't trust her. I couldn't fuck with somebody that would do some shit like that. Then Rita started actin—" Brick was saying until Sameria cut him off.

"Weren't you and my dad friends?" Sameria asked.

"Yea, and I told him to leave yo' mom alone, but he loved her, and love got him killed. Sean didn't want to believe that she was fucking with Jigga. Me and even his momma tried to tell him, but Susie said it was a lie, so he took her word over ours. When—"

"What does Rita have to do with that?" I asked.

"Rita went to meet Sean to pick up some work like she did many of times, but this time, Jigga was laying in the back seat of the car. Since Jigga was fucking Rita too, he was able to get in her ear and tell her that if they got rid of Sean, he could take over and they could finally be together."

"That's why they stopped talking," Me and Sameria both said with it all coming together and starting to make sense.

As Brick started to tell us everything that happened, a lot of stuff started to make sense. Sameria told me about what her grandma told her, but that was just the part about Jigga fucking with her momma behind her dad's back. She didn't say anything about my momma being involved. With how close Sean and Brick were back in the day, I'm not surprised, but what I don't understand is with how crazy Rita was over Brick, why she would risk it fucking with somebody else? That may be something that I may never know because I have no intentions on ever talking to her again.

"I know this is a lot, and I'm not trying to make no excuse for the way I mishandled the situation. Even with all that, I should have been there for you. I know that I can't take it back, but I want to start from here to make shit right," Brick pleaded.

"What did that lady do to Pumpkin?" I asked, just wanting to be nosy.

"She was fucking with Pumpkin's sister's man," Brick replied.

"I'm willing to try to get to know you, but you can't

bring that lady around," I said, already knowing how Chaos and Scar would react if they knew who she was.

"Alright, I can do that."

"Let's go and open the gifts, so I can go home," I said, standing up and with Brick and Sameria by my sides, we made our way back to the party.

24

SCAR

"Even though I don't like the bitch, when you start to avoidin' going home, that's a fuckin' problem. You pay bills there. You should always feel comfortable goin' to yo' own fuckin' house," Pumpkin said as we sat in the kitchen at her house while I ate.

"P, Fe not just some bitch. That's been my girl for a minute, and I was trying to make this shit work."

"You can't make something work when the otha muthafucka ain't. This shit alone should be enough," Pumpkin said, handing me back the papers I showed her.

"I'll be back," I said, standing up to throw my plate away and go holla at Felicia.

Pumpkin didn't respond, but I could hear her flickin' her lighter, lighting up a cigarette. I made my way out the house and my phone started ringing. Felicia and I were barely hanging on and two weeks ago after we left Cina's baby shower, she came to me telling me that her momma, Nina, needed to stay with us for two days. I didn't want her at my house, but because the lady didn't have nowhere else to go, I let her come. Now I know that I should have told her to figure something else out.

I made it to the house and Zai and Nina's cars were in my driveway like they pay bills at this bitch. I told Felicia that everybody needed to be gone by the time I got here and clearly, she thought that I was fucking playing. I want shit organized and in its place, but with muthafuckas in yo' house, that ain't easy. Throwing my car into park, I jumped out and went into the house. As I walked in, I could smell fucking cigarettes and that was the final fucking straw.

I don't even let Pumpkin smoke in my house, now Nina thinks that she can even after I told her old ass she couldn't. As I came into the house, all eyes were on me. I snatched Nina's cigarette out of her hand and threw it out the front door. Just missing Pumpkin that was coming up the walkway. I would ask her why she's here, but right now that don't even matter.

"Y'all go to fucking go," I said as I made my way back in the house.

"Momma, I'll call you later," Zai said, getting up to leave.

"Naw, you gon' take her with you," I said, unplugging Nina's oxygen machine to speed up the process.

"Baby, calm down. You can't put my mom out. She can't go with Zai," Fe pleaded.

"Yo' ass can go with her too," I said, which surprised everybody in the room.

"What the fuck do you mean I can go with her too? I'm not going no fucking where and neither is my momma."

"Oh, y'all bitches gon' get the fuck up out of here!"

Pumpkin spat as she sat down in my chair, making Nina look at Fe, waiting for her to do something.

"P, chill," I said, looking over at her.

"When the fuck was you gon' tell me you were failing school? And I know yo' ass still been stealing. The fact that you let yo' momma smoke in my house just shows where the fuck we stand. You take whatever you want out this bitch, but you got to go," I said, pushing Felicia off of me.

"I... I was gon' talk to you about school today, and I'm done. I promise you that I'm done with that shit. I won't do it again," Felicia pleaded.

"No, the bitch not, she lying again," Pumpkin said.

"You just gon' let these people come in yo' house and just talk about us like we ain't sittin' here! Put his ass out! Call the fucking police and let them decide who the fuck has to go!" Nina yelled loud enough for my neighbors to hear her.

"Call the police, huh? Fuck what I said about taking whatever you want, get fuck out my house," I said, snatching the oxygen off of Nina and throwing the machine in the front yard.

Once I did that, Felicia knew that I was no longer playing. I know that Felicia knew that shit hasn't been right with us for a while. Our history made me feel like I had to stay with her because I owed her. But fuck that and this bitch. They both can get the fuck on. Once I threw the oxygen machin,e that was Pumpkin's que to start throwing everything that belonged to Nina or Fe into my front yard.

"Really? You gon' let Pumpkin just come in here and

throw my shit in the front yard?" Felicia screamed as I made my way upstairs.

"Bitch, be lucky I ain't breaking yo' fucking neck. Not only was you out here embarrassing me and shit, but I know you took that fucking money out my safe," I spat through gritted teeth.

As I turned around to face Felicia on the stairs, her eyes got big as hell because I know she didn't see that coming. When the money came up missing, I thought I was trippin'. I doubled back to make sure that I didn't put it somewhere else or leave it in one of the hiding spots at the traps. The bitch even helped me look for the money and then later that night, the bitch's niece knocked her purse over and the money fell out. I didn't say shit, but I knew that it was my money.

When she was doing the stealing shit to get by while I was away, I didn't like it, but I wasn't trippin'. Once I came home, we were supposed to be getting shit right. And once I got my money right, all that shit was supposed to be done, but her ass just couldn't stop. Once I knew that she would steal from me, I knew that I couldn't trust her. Pumpkin always told me that she would, but I didn't want to believe that shit, not my bitch. I fucked up, but today is the day.

"Can we please just talk?" Felicia cried.

"It ain't shit to talk about. Get the fuck out, Felicia," I said, snatching the keys to the house out of her pocket.

"Scar!" Felicia begged.

"Felicia, come on. You don't need him," Zai said, pulling her away.

It ain't shit that we need to talk about. I don't give a

fuck about how none of her people feel about me and the way shit played out. Yea, that bitch was there for me while I was down bad, but once I got right, I made sure that bitch was right. I went above and beyond to make sure that she was good. I did shit that even my people told me not to do, but because she was my girl, I made sure she was straight. In the end, I should have left her ass alone a long time ago, but it is what it is. I'll never let another bitch get close enough to me to fuck me over again.

With Pumpkin's help throwing their shit out, Felicia and her momma were gone within an hour and everything that they didn't get will be going to the Goodwill. I hired a cleaning service that should be here any moment. Pumpkin was downstairs celebrating that Fe and I are over. Music was blasting and she was singing along to every song. I just want to her to stay here while these people clean, so I can go and pick up some money. As I made my way downstairs, Antonio was calling my phone.

"What's up?" I asked as I answered the phone.

"You coming? I need to get to the hospital with Tay," Antonio said.

"I'm on my way. That probably ain't yo' fucking baby anyways," I said and hung up on him.

It ain't no secret, everybody knows that bitch be fucking on everybody. I would ask Pumpkin if she going to the hospital, but I already know the answer. I'm sure that he didn't even waste his time calling her. Maybe one day she'll put her pride to the side and see her grandchild, but today ain't the day. That would explain why she is still at my house and done started drinking, making herself comfortable like she plans on staying for a while.

"I'm staying here tonight," Pumpkin said as I let the cleaning ladies in and made my way out.

I went and picked up my money from Antonio then got something to eat and went to talk to Ricardo. Pulling up to Pumpkin's my phone started ringing with a number I didn't recognize. I answered and when I heard the voice on the other end, I started to hang up because I don't want to hear shit this bitch could have to say.

"I know your mad right now, but Felicia just got arrested." Zai said.

"I don't care. What the fuck are you calling me for? I ain't got shit for that bitch. That money she stole, she should have saved some."

Click.

I hung up on her and made my way into the house. I'm surprised this nigga is here. Since he been off GPS, he been at the house with Cina every chance he gets. Ain't nothin' gon' keep them apart, not even a fucking restraining order. If they get caught, that nigga knows he's going back to jail. After that bullshit that went down at the baby shower a few weeks back, Ricardo doesn't want Cina doing nothing. He was trippin' with Pumpkin about how she acted, but Pumpkin made it clear she didn't have to explain herself to him, and she hasn't either. She won't even tell us why she jumped on that lady.

"You good?" Ricardo asked as I walked in the living room.

"Yea, shit. Fuck that bitch," I replied.

"Where Cina?" I asked, surprised she ain't here.

"She went to have dinner with her dad and grandma."

"I know you said to wait until you could do it with me,

but I want to get her people now," I said, referring to Lil Miller.

"This is personal, and I need to handle that on my own."

"What about her momma?"

"I'll handle her too."

25

SAMERIA

"Come outside right quick, I want to show you some-thin'," Yasir said and disconnected the call.

Closing my laptop, I got up and slipped on my slides so I could go and see what he wants. Yasir knew my situation in my dorm, so he asked me to come stay with him. He already knows how his cousin gets down and the bitch gets worse and worse every day. I tried to talk to her and that bitch still couldn't get it together. It got so bad that I was ready to go and stay with Susie. I go to the dorm when I'm supposed to meet my momma, other than that, I'm at his house. And that is working out because he lives across the street from my new job.

"You got a new truck?" I asked, confused on why he called me to come see his new truck. He's always switching up trucks. I looked at the GX 460 in the driveway.

"Naw, this you," Yasir said, handing me the keys and kissing me on the lips.

"For real?" I asked as I started to circle the truck.

We were talking last night, and I told Yasir that this was the truck that I wanted but didn't think that meant he was going to wake up and go get it for me. I've been feeling like a burden by having to depend on him getting me to and from school. Whenever I say anything about it, Yasir cuts me off and assures me that he has me. Yasir is always buying me something and the last time I tried to tell him that he didn't have to, he went off and shit went left, so I'm not about to go there today. He has told me that whatever I need, he'll make sure that I get it, and he hasn't let me down yet.

With everything that I've been dealing with, finding out the truth about my dad's murder, Yasir has been here for me. Whenever I need him, he comes through. Half the time I don't even have to ask, and he just shows up. Having somebody to lean on that I don't have to ask to be here for me means the most. He knows how me and my momma's relationship is and if I ever need to vent, he's always here just to listen, and I never feel like I'm being judged.

I've met his parents and the rest of his family, and they have let me in with open arms. It was a lot to get use to because his family spends a lot of time together and that is not something that I'm familiar with. It's nice to be around them because I never experienced that before. My momma's family is all fucked up. I can't remember the last time I even seen any of them. My dad's family tried but ever since that day at my grandma's, I haven't talked to any of them, but I still text Mikki here and there. So being around his family, a real family, is cool.

I hugged and thanked Yasir over and over. It's crazy because when I met him, I didn't think that we would go anywhere. I wasn't interested but having somebody like him in my life has been refreshing. When I got back from Denver, I felt bad for the night that I spent with Zion. I damn sure didn't plan for things to play out like they did.

I was going to tell Yasir, but after talking about with Cina, I decided that might not be a good idea. Losing him over something that didn't mean anything wouldn't be worth it. I promised myself that it would never happen again and pretended that it never did. Zion calls every once in a while, but I have never answered because we were done for good now. I'm happy where I'm at, and he's just a part of my past that I plan to keep there.

"Go get dressed. Let's go get something to eat," Yasir said, breaking our embrace.

"I can't, I have to be to work in a few hours," I said while looking at Zay and I can already tell that he doesn't want me to go.

"Alright," Zay replied dry as hell.

"Tomorrow I'm off. We can do something then," I assured him.

The time that we have together was already short, but since I been working, it's been even shorter. Zay keeps asking me to quit, but I don't know about that. I need a job, so that I can cover my own ass. Right now, I'm just stacking my money in case of an emergency.

For me, it's more than what he does for me financially that makes me stay with Zay. If he stopped doing anything for me, I would still want to be with him. Zay's phone started ringing, and we made our way into the house and mine followed. It was my momma. I haven't talked to her in a few days, so I decided to answer.

"Hey, mom," I said into the phone as I picked up my

laptop to finish looking for a dress for Yasir's birthday party next weekend.

"Hey. I didn't get a statement from the school. You need to check on that. I need to set up a payment plan for this semester," my momma said, sounding tired as hell.

"Yasir took care of it. There is no balance due."

"He paid the whole thing? What about your books?"

"He took care of it."

"I guess his old ass is good for something. You need to stay with him until you finish school.

"Yea, alright, ma."

"Don't *yea, alright* me. You need to at least be getting something out of it. What was them other niggas doing for you? Buying you some shoes, gettin' yo' nails painted? Fuck all that, yo' education is something that you'll always have even when that's over."

"You are planning for us to break up?" I asked, getting irritated with the way this conversation is going.

"Well, nothing lasts forever."

"Alright, mom. I got to go get ready for work," I said, trying to rush her off the phone.

Yasir trying to get in good with me was going behind my back and doing shit for my mom. Paying her rent, getting her car fixed, just little shit here and there. Trying to show her the type of man he is. It sounds good and it's sweet that he was trying to show me how much he cared being there for my family, but I put an end to all that because the type of person my momma is, she'll take advantage as long as she can. Next thing you know, she'd be calling asking for shit just because she thought she could.

"What time do you get off?" Yasir asked as I ended the call with my mom.

"Eleven," I said in between yawning.

"You don't have to work. When I tell you that I got you, do you believe me?" Yasir asked.

"Yea, but Yasir, this is good experience, so that when I finish school, it will be easier for me to get a job."

"Ain't no buts. I want you to just focus on school and you can't do that if you over there half the week. I know what yo' situation is and you don't want to have to depend on yo' momma. I got that, but I ain't ya momma," Yasir said as he wrapped his hands around my waist.

Yasir moved my hair and started placing soft kisses on my neck. He didn't want me to get a job from the beginning and I understood his point of why, but that doesn't take away from the reason why I needed one. We have been over this a million times, and I don't think that he will ever get it. He comes from money and his parents and my momma are nothing alike.

"What happened to you wanting to take another class this semester? You think that you're going to be able to handle five classes and working, Sameria?" Zay asked.

I didn't answer, but he is right. I want to take more classes, so that I can finish earlier. The sooner the better. College is cool, and I love the new experiences that I'm getting, but finishing and getting my career started would be even better.

"I know you heard me. Just think about it," Zay said as he kissed me on the cheek and made his way down the hallway to his office.

～

"Do you know her?" Another CNA named Brittany asked me.

"She's here to see Mrs. Gaines. I think that's one of her granddaughters," I said, looking over at the lady that was staring in our direction.

"She's been up here every day this week. Nobody comes and sees their maw maw this much. That bitch is always staring you down whenever you're here," Brittany said.

"Who y'all talking about?" Christina asked as she walked into the supply closet me and Brittany are in.

"She did ask me were you here yesterday, so clearly she knows you," Christina stated, which caught my attention.

"Mrs. Gaines probably wanted to know was I here. I always go and sit with her. She doesn't like none of y'all, so she always asks am I here. I'm sure that's why she asked for me."

Brittany and Christina talked about the lady across the hall as I texted Cina back. She's at the hospital, so hopefully she'll be having the baby soon. We always sit here and talk whenever we don't have anything else to do. I made my way out the closet and down the hall because a patient pressed the call button.

"Are you Sameria?" Someone asked from behind me.

"Yes, that's my name."

Turning around, it was the lady who always comes to visit Mrs. Gaines. She's a pretty, light skin woman with reddish brown curly hair and a face full of freckles. She was thicker than a snicker and definitely from here because she has a thick country ass accent.

"Do you know who I am?" The woman asked.

"I guess you're related to or friends with Mrs. Gaines," I said, getting confused by the way that this bitch is mugging me.

"I'm Mrs. Taylor," the woman said, showing me her wedding ring.

"Okay, Mrs. Taylor, how can I help you?"

"So, you just gon' sit there and act like you don't know who I am. Well, let me break it down for you. I'm Yasir Taylor's wife! Do you get the picture now, sweetie?" The woman said, raising her voice, catching everybody in the hallway's attention and there were at least ten people out here.

"You're his what?" I asked, still confused because to be honest, I really can't believe this shit.

The woman pulled out her phone showing me pictures of Yasir and her and pictures of him and a little girl that looks like her and a little boy that looks like him. As she scrolled through her phone, I was speechless. I didn't know what to say. There damn sure were no signs that he was with somebody else. We live together and whenever we are not around each other, we're either texting or on the phone.

"We have a family, and I'm not about to let some broke ass out of town bitch fuck up what we have. I know you're trying to act surprised like you didn't know about me but let me tell you this. He is my husband and will always be my husband. There is nothing that you can do to ever come in between what we hav—"

"Have him, he's all you, baby," I said and walked away to go and check on my patient.

I'd be lying if I said I wasn't hurt. The pain that I'm feeling in my chest is evident of that. The tears that started to fall, I wiped them away and took a deep breath, praying, begging God to get me through this shift. I got my patient together and made my way back to the bathroom because I needed a minute to get myself together. As I locked the bathroom stall behind me, my tears just started falling. I squatted down, buried my face into my hands and just let it all out.

Just when I thought that things had turned around, and I finally found a nigga that was all about me and didn't want anybody else, I find out all of that was a lie. This nigga took me around his family, introduced me to his dying grandma and the whole time he has a whole family on the other side of town. Mrs. Gaines talks a lot about her family. She has pictures of that lady and her kids all over her room.

She's always talking about her granddaughter and how they have such a beautiful family, but the whole time I never imagined that it was with Yasir. Yasir has come up here to bring me food. Mrs. Gaines even met Yasir in the lobby several times and never said anything about knowing him. As I cried into my hands, I could hear Brittany and Christina on the other side of the stall talking to me, but I'm not hearing anything their saying.

For once, I thought that I had one. I thought that things were working out for me finally. I saw myself being with Yasir for the long run. I thought we had a future together and one day would have a family. Clearly, that all was a dream because I can't start a family with a man that already has one. I got myself together because I couldn't stay in here. I have to make it through this shift.

It was a struggle, but I made it through my shift. Cina was still in labor, but Pumpkin is keeping me posted. I talked to Cina a few times, but she's so high, she probably won't remember we talked. As I went to punch out, my supervisor stopped me and said that she needed to talk to me.

"I received a call from your boyfriend. He said that he had been trying to reach you. I'm sorry to tell you this, but your sister was shot earlier today," my supervisor, Janice, said.

I heard what she said, but I didn't respond. She kept asking me if I'm okay, but I still hadn't responded. I'm trying to wrap my mind around what she just said to me.

"Is she okay? Did she make it?" I asked.

"I'm sorry, Sameria, she didn't. Would you like me to take you the hospital, so you can be with your family?" Janice asked.

"No but thank you."

"If you need anything, please don't hesitate to reach out to me and let me know," Janice stated.

I clocked out and made my way across the street to the house. Luckily, Yasir wasn't here, but his wife was sitting in the driveway. The bitch hasn't said anything, she's just sitting there. If she knows about me then she knew that I was staying here. Right now, with all that's on my mind, I don't have the time or the energy to argue with this bitch, so it will be her best bet to not say shit to me.

My phone started ringing. I checked it to make sure that it wasn't my momma, but it was Yasir. We don't have anything to discuss, so I sent him to voicemail for what felt like the hundredth time. I tried to call my momma again, but she didn't answer. I picked up my laptop and my books for school, everything else I don't care about. I'm leaving, but I not until I get one more thing.

Making my way to Yasir's 's office. I entered the code and the door beeped, letting me in. I entered another code to separate the book shelf that gave me access to his safe. I filled my pockets, the emptied space in my purse and back pack with stacks of money. This isn't some shit that I would do because I'm not this type of bitch, but after this bullshit, I feel that I deserve this and more. I made my way out the house. At the front door, I was met by two niggas in ski masks who both pulled out their heat on me as I stepped on the welcome mat.

To Be Continued...

CPSIA information can be obtained
at www.ICGtesting.com
Printed in the USA
LVHW031823230419
615253LV00003B/477